FOREVER BE MINE

Love in London- Book 4

LAUREN SMITH

For anyone who's dared to risk it all for love. This story is for you.

The last thing in the world Celia Lynton wanted to do was attend a garden party at her uncle's English estate, but it was a matter of life or death. At least, it felt like it was. If she'd had her way, she would have been catching a late matinee at the nearest theater or tucked away in the corner of a cozy coffee shop reading a book.

Instead, she was living out some Jane Austen fantasy, minus the historical clothes, of course. It was 2019 after all, but bloody hell, all those men and women wandering around tea tables, gossiping about one another and the state of England—it was definitely not how she wanted to spend her day.

Her uncle, the Earl of Pembroke, was a powerful player in the English political climate, especially in the House of Lords. Being at this party was crucial for her family. Just a few months ago, her father had lost their entire fortune in a poor investment. Recently, they'd moved into a tiny cottage on her uncle's estate, and the life she and her younger brother, Matthew, had been accustomed to had vanished overnight. This party offered her a chance to help her family, but that didn't mean she had to like it.

She'd managed to escape the party for a few minutes and now lingered in the doorway to one of the many guest rooms at her uncle's country manor house. She watched her brother scribble away in a notebook, muttering softly to himself.

She was here for him and she was about to sacrifice everything for him. She loved Matthew, and as his older sister, it was her duty to look out for him. He was only fifteen, but he was a genius when it came to science and mathematics. However, he had problems. For the longest time they'd struggled to understand why he was doing so poorly in other subjects and why he had trouble socializing with others. They'd recently learned that he was on the autism spectrum—high functioning, and he aslo suffered from dyslexia and other issues.

"Matthew, are you coming down to the party?" she asked quietly.

Her brother shook his head. His gold hair glowing in the afternoon sunlight as it poured through the tall bay windows, making him look so young. But he was fifteen, a young man, no longer a child. Matthew sat at an antique desk, several textbooks spread out before him, completely lost in a world of numbers and equations. A small smile graced Celia's lips, but her heart ached. He was the reason she was about to do something that would change her life forever. Something she would forever keep a secret from him because she never wanted him to feel guilty.

Somewhere in the midst of the party was a handsome twenty-seven year old Scottish man named Callum Radcliffe. She'd met him a decade ago at one of these garden parties, and they'd formed a deep friendship. Today, he would propose to her. And even though she didn't love him, even though she burned for another, she would say yes.

Matthew had been removed from Eton College when he'd gotten into a fight with a few of the boys there who'd been bullying him because of his autism and dyslexia. The fight had been bad enough but one of the boys Matthew had quarreled with was the son of an influential viscount who was a generous donor to Eton. Matthew therefore was asked to leave. The real problem was that what Matthew needed, a school which focused heavily on math and science, her family could no longer afford. While the National Health Service in England paid for medical care and students could attend free state schools, Matthew had been accepted to a special academy that had a steep tuition not covered by the National Health Service.

Ravenswood Academy was a school which specialized in math and science fields and they offered even better specialists to help with Matthew's issues than Eton did. It was just the sort of place which could offer Matthew the type of education which would get him into Cambridge and connected with the right people who valued his special abilities in math and science. They had offered Matthew a spot starting in just two months, but her parents could no longer afford the tuition.

Celia had hoped her new position in London at Morton & Ridings Architecture would have provided enough to pay for Matthew's schooling, but she was a new hire with a entry-level salary. In fact, she was convinced she'd only been hired because of her social connections with no consideration towards her talent as an architect.

Much had changed so quickly. Between losing their family home and worrying about how to pay for Ravenswood, their world had been completely altered, and not even her uncle, who had given them the run of the tiny three-bedroom cottage on his estate, could be confided in for this particular problem.

Uncle Edward had stepped in and paid off the massive debts her father had accumulated and saved them from facing lawsuits and creditors. But his generosity could only stretch so far. Neither Celia nor her parents wanted to ask him to pay for Matthew's tuition. Besides her parents were too busy keeping up appearances and trying to see if their social connections might pay off in some way. But it seemed the only way Celia could help was by marrying Callum. As the next in line to an earldom, he needed to marry well and have at least one son.

Celia cringed at the thought of what she and Callum had secretly agreed to. A marriage of convenience. It was still commonplace in parts of Britain's upper society, but she'd never expected to be involved in such an arrangement. Callum was sweet, good looking, and ready to help fund Matthew's schooling. Although they were good friends, he didn't love her and could never love her, not in that way. His partner, Bryson Verne, was still a secret he kept from his parents, but one he'd have to give up. Even though the queen's cousin had recently married his partner, Callum feared his parents wouldn't accept him for who he truly was.

He loved his parents, loved his home, and he knew his duty. If he didn't produce an heir, the estate would someday pass on to a distant cousin he barely knew. So a month ago he and Celia had come up with a plan. They would get married. Matthew's education would be assured, and Callum could do right by his family and position. All Celia had to do was produce an heir...

She cleared her throat, ignoring the uncomfortable tightness that threatened to choke her. "Matthew?"

"Hmm?" Her little brother didn't bother looking up from his studies. He didn't hear the laughter and music coming through the windows. Or if he did, he didn't care.

"The party," she reminded him gently. "Try to come for at least a few minutes. Tristan and Carter would love to see you."

"It's very loud. I don't like it."

"You can go to the garden. It's quieter there."

"Okay…" Matthew's distracted reply told her that he would forget about the party as soon as Celia left the room. With a sigh, she left him to his world of numbers and went to rejoin the party. She paused halfway down the stairs, looking out of the tall window that faced the gardens beyond. Her heart stopped.

Strolling at the edge of the crowd was a tall blond-haired man wearing a navy-blue suit that clung to him like a second skin. His leonine grace and exquisite masculine features drew the eye of every woman in sight. Heads actually turned as he walked toward Uncle Edward's house and then stopped at the end of the crowd, keeping himself slightly distant from the other guests.

Carter Martin.

Her heart skipped a painful beat. She pressed a hand to the glass, feeling the sun warm her palm as her soul shook deep inside her. Carter was the man she'd always imagined being with before she fell asleep every night. His arms wrapped around her, his lips brushing her ear as he whispered good night before she slipped into the most perfect dreams. She'd known him for as long as she could remember, but he was the son of her uncle's steward for the Pembroke estate and worked as a junior steward. That made things impossible.

Her uncle would forbid the two of them becoming involved, and her parents certainly wouldn't allow it. And if they had chosen to sneak around, he could have lost his job, possibly his father as well, their chances of employment damaged forever. She could only imagine things ending badly for Carter, and the last thing she wanted to do was hurt him.

There were bloody stupid, archaic, backward prejudices at play, but that didn't change the fact that she couldn't spend the rest of her life with him. Certainly not now, when her life was crumbling around her. Desperate as it was, Callum was the only way she could protect her brother, which meant she'd never know what it meant to be loved by Carter, never be the woman who won his wicked smiles or felt his body cover hers in a dark bedroom as passion burned hot and fiery between them.

"Celia?" Callum's voice drifted up from the bottom of the stairs.

She dropped her hand from the window, turning away from the man she would always long for, and faced the man who was her future.

"Everything all right with Matthew?" he asked as she joined him at the bottom of the stairs.

She nodded. "He's deep in his textbooks."

"As usual," Callum replied with a gentle chuckle. Then he glanced around before he leaned into her. "Your parents are waiting in the drawing room. I thought I could propose to you there—make it official, if you like." He offered her his arm, and she accepted it, her heart pounding with nerves as she nodded.

Callum seemed to notice her pain and paused. "You don't have to do this, you know. I could find someone else to..." He blushed.

"No, it's okay. This is best for everyone. You're a good friend, and that's important in a marriage. We'll be happy."

His eyes filled with an echoing sorrow. "Content, perhaps. We both know what we're giving up."

He understood what it was like to sacrifice. He would never be able to marry for love either, and Bryson knew that it would soon be over between them. No matter how normal it might be among the aristocracy to have affairs, she and Callum both agreed that marriage as an institution had to be respected, even more so once a child became involved.

They were sacrificing so much. Surely they both needed time to—

Carter's face flashed across her mind. A sudden idea burst inside her, brilliant and full of hope, like fireworks. Would it work? Would Callum agree?

"Callum...if we do this, I need a month to..." She struggled for composure as a rush of painful emotions tightened her chest before she continued. "I would like a month to myself first. I would like to leave England, to have some time with someone I care about before we make an official announcement—outside of our parents, I mean."

He nodded slowly. "I was thinking the same. Bryson and I would appreciate the time with each other as well. He understands my situation, but...we need time."

Celia exhaled a shaky breath, relieved that Callum felt the same. They both needed one last taste of what it felt like to be loved before they did what duty required of them.

They reached the tearoom, and Callum ushered her inside. A connecting door led to the drawing room, where her parents were waiting to eavesdrop. Callum faced her, taking her hands in his.

"Ready?" he whispered.

She gave a shaky nod. Callum eased down onto one knee.

Let the show begin.

"Celia Lynton, for ten years we have been close friends, and in that time we've only grown closer. I cannot picture a day in my life without you by my side. Would you do me the honor of becoming my wife?"

Celia's heart leapt into her throat. All she could think was that she was twenty-five, yet it felt like her life was already ending.

"Celia?" Callum Radcliffe stared up at her with

those dark-brown eyes any person in their right mind would swoon over.

But he wasn't the man she dreamed about at night. He wasn't the man she'd fantasized would be on one knee during what should have been the most perfect moment of her life. He wasn't Carter Martin.

"I...yes." She almost faltered on the word she'd promised she would say. Suddenly things spun around her as the doors to the tearoom burst open and her parents, Bernadette and Hensley Lynton, rushed in.

"Oh, congratulations!" her mother cooed and gave her a light hug that lacked any real warmth. Her father smiled proudly and offered a hand to Callum so he could pull him in and slap him on the back.

"So glad to see you two finally settling things," Hensley announced.

Celia looked between Callum and her parents, still uncertain. He was a good man, she knew that, and he would make a fine husband, at least as a companion. But they both loved other people.

This is what is expected of me. But I had dreams.

"She's overwhelmed with happiness, aren't you, dear?" Her mother gave her a hard nudge in the ribs.

The reality of the moment began to sink in. She'd been looking forward to her work in London at the architecture firm, but now she would have to add social duties to her life as a future countess in Scotland. And she always had Matthew to consider, since she couldn't trust her parents to put the needs of their youngest child above their own.

"Perhaps it's just nerves?" Callum suggested, his eyes dark with concern. But he understood what she was feeling, that sense of hope fading like a dying star, burning out far away in endless space. They were both giving up their hopes of being with the person they loved in order to help their families.

"Yes, she's nervous," her mother cut in. "But she's thrilled, of course!"

Celia stared mutely at her mother, then at Callum. How was it that her life was going on without her in it? It was like she was trapped in a nightmare where she couldn't move, couldn't speak.

Callum grinned in pretend relief and clasped her hands in his and leaned down to brush his lips over hers. They were soft and warm, but there was no wild spark, no passion to excite her. He tried to kiss her a second longer, to make it look convincing, but when she didn't respond he gently pulled back.

"I suppose we should get back to the party. Everyone will be missing us," Callum said to her parents. "I should like to request that our engagement be kept a secret for a time. I believe a month before we announce it publicly would be in order."

Her father was still smiling broadly. "Of course, of course."

Celia's throat tightened as she forced a bright smile back on her face. Callum and her father left the room, but she was rooted to the floor on a one-hundred-year-old oriental carpet. She knew it was 2019, so why did she feel like a woman trapped in the eighteenth century?

"Celia," her mother hissed. "You will *not* mess this up for your father and me, do you understand? Callum will someday be the Earl of Cavanagh. You'll be a countess. It's more than your father and I could ever dream of. Our family needs this, not to mention poor Matthew."

It seemed, despite most of England joining the world in the twenty-first century, some things hadn't really changed in the last thousand years. Men still held fancy titles and still needed heirs to continue their lines. Which ultimately made women like her a commodity.

"Yes, Mother. I understand." Celia repeated the words that were to become the nails in her invisible coffin. It was so easy for the rest of the world to do whatever they liked, marry and fall in love with whomever they chose.

"Mum, I'd like to go to Italy and see Aunt Holly before we make the engagement public." Holly was one of the few members of Celia's family whom she actually liked. It was a small and exclusive group comprised of her brother, her cousin Tristan, and Holly.

Her mother didn't immediately say no, but the grim line of her over-red lips wasn't a good sign either. "For the entire month?" she asked.

"I need this, Mum." If her mother dared to try to stop her, she would go anyway. But after a moment of internal debate, she seemed to relent.

"I'll check with your father, of course, but I imagine he'll agree. You can take his jet." It wasn't really her father's jet, rather it was Uncle Edward's, but the Earl of Pembroke was fond of his sister and loaned them the use of it whenever they needed it.

"Thank you," Celia murmured. A single month away from a future she didn't want and couldn't avoid. It would have to be enough.

"Take a minute to compose yourself, then join your fiancé at the party." Her mother left her alone, and Celia sank down in the nearest chair.

Her red gown flowed around her like the petals of a rose, but it felt like a lie to wear a gown that her family could no longer afford. Later this evening, the rented gown would be returned to the store with no one the wiser. It was one more falsity among a dozen others in her life.

Struck with this thought, the tears came at last. Hard sobs choked her so that she couldn't catch her breath. Until the moment Callum proposed, she hadn't wanted to accept that this nightmare was real, that she would have to give up the last real dream she'd clung to her in life.

To be with Carter.

She took several deep breaths to calm herself and

studied her reflection in the mirror. Her blonde hair was down around her shoulders in perfect romantic waves, even though her mother had been most insistent she wear it up. Her eyes looked a bit red, and the tip of her nose was red too. It was far too obvious she'd been crying.

"Bloody hell," she cursed, then smiled a little.

She blamed her cousin, Tristan, for her inner turmoil. Future earl, the tabloids' beloved bad boy, and current besotted boyfriend of Celia's new best friend, Kat. Come to think of it, she blamed Kat as well. If it hadn't been for Kat's charming American ways, Celia wouldn't have spent so much time with the couple, which meant that she could have kept her distance from Carter, which would have made this easier. Given that Carter was Tristan's best friend, it meant he was around altogether too much and yet never enough.

So it was really Tristan and Kat's fault that she couldn't come to terms with letting Carter go. Even though it was the right thing to do. She had no right to claim him. As a steward's son, he would never have the kind of money their family needed. That Matthew needed.

Celia dabbed at her eyes and collected herself, just as her mother had instructed. She walked through her uncle's grand house, preparing to face England's high society once again. But as she took the entrance through to the servants' hall, a shortcut she'd learned when she was seven, she caught sight of Carter again through one of the windows.

He still stood facing the crowds, milling about the tea tables in the gardens. The man looked perfect. Perfect and completely unattainable. He was twenty-six, and with his gorgeous heartbreaker looks, he was catching the eye of every lady, even the married ones. He watched the crowds, and raked a hand through his dark-gold hair, a habit he did only when he was bothered by something. Celia couldn't help but wonder what preoccupied him. According to Tristan, he could have any woman he wanted. The thought made her stomach churn with jealousy, but she certainly had no right to tell him who he could be with.

She left through the door that led from the servants' quarters to the gardens. Celia didn't dare step out into the light and risk being seen.

Take Carter to Italy. Have a taste of the life you've always wanted with the man you've always desired. One last hurrah before it ends. Do it, or you'll regret it.

She'd grown up watching him as a young boy, then as a lanky awkward teen, and finally a flirtatious young man. Now he was simply irresistible. She'd been tied to him like how a violin belonged with its bow her entire life, wanting nothing more than to make sweet music together, yet they'd never dared to play a note.

She knew he cared about her, possibly even loved her, though neither of them had ever dared breathe a word of it. He was too responsible, too dutiful, to ever cross that line. They'd kissed only once in their lives, the only time he'd ever lost control around her. But she'd tasted his longing for her in that kiss, felt the echoing loneliness and love for her in it. It had shaken her to her core and her even more afraid of her own feelings.

"Carter?" She spoke his name quietly, not wanting to draw attention from the crowds.

He spun around, lips parted, gray eyes haunted and yet so beautiful. Carter had the sort of masculine beauty that could stop a woman in her tracks, and yet he seemed entirely unaware of his effect. That only made him all the more desirable. She trembled as she thought of having him all to herself for a month.

Just the two of us. If he'll let me.

"Celia? What's the matter?"

Rather than answer him, she reached out, grabbed

his tie, and dragged him back into the house, slamming the door behind them. The sounds of the party were muted, and the servants' quarters were dim except for a distant light from the other end of the hall. Carter gripped her shoulders, and she shivered at the feel of his hands on her bare skin. These little moments were never enough. She struggled to remember what she wanted to tell him and, more importantly, what she wanted to ask him.

She hesitated, swallowed hard. "I have to tell you something."

"Celia, what is it? Talk to me." She could feel the tension radiating off him. One could only wonder what dire news he expected to hear.

She nodded to herself and continued.

"Callum proposed today. My parents are already talking about announcing the engagement in a month." Unable to meet his gaze, she glanced down.

"I see," was all Carter said.

"It's for the best, you understand. If I marry him, he will pay for Matthew's tuition to Ravenswood Academy. They have specialists and a great program focusing on math and science which he could really benefit from."

"And you said yes." His deep voice was as rich as brandy, but she heard the note of worry buried within.

Celia stared deep into his eyes, then slowly nodded. "I did. My job doesn't pay enough to cover even a quarter of Matthew's tuition."

A stray tear trickled down her cheek. They were trapped. Callum was having to live a lie, she would have to marry for money, and the people they loved had to be abandoned.

"Poor Callum." She thought of how happy he and Bryson had been for the last two years, but they'd had to keep their love a secret from his parents.

"Poor Callum?" Carter growled. "You talk about

saving Matthew and worrying about Callum, but what about *you*? Don't do this, Celia. Tell me you'll stop it. He's a nice enough bloke, but you can't marry him, even if it is for Matthew. You won't be happy."

"I *have* to." She pleaded with her eyes for him to understand, tracing her fingers along his tie, her fingertips touching the silver tie clip. She was unable to resist touching him.

Carter's eyes warmed, his head dipping toward her, the suggestion of a kiss before he pulled away and looked into her face with a calmness that steadied her.

"I'll find a way to help Matthew. Give me time."

"No." She pressed her hand against his warm chest. "There isn't time. He's already been accepted to the academy, and Callum's already paid for his first semester."

The wounded expression in Carter's eyes nearly undid her. He'd wanted to be the one to help Matthew, she knew that, but it wasn't possible.

"But you don't love him. You can't marry someone you don't love."

Her laugh was hollow. "Since when have I ever had a choice in who I love?"

Carter nodded at the party through the windows by the servants' door. She caught a glimpse of her cousin Tristan and his girlfriend Kat. They were dancing together while a Beatles cover band played "Yellow Submarine." Tristan spun Kat, and she laughed in delight. Nothing in the world was stopping those two from being together.

"If they can, *we* can," Carter insisted, lifting her hand up to brush his lips over her knuckles. He seemed so certain, so sure as he spoke, yet she saw clear desperation in his eyes as he seemed to realize this was his last chance. He couldn't accept the fact that it was already too late.

His eyes were twin pools reflecting the overcast

sky above, and it made her dizzy to gaze into them. At that moment, she felt she and Carter were caught in a glass bubble, just the two of them, their hunger building like a wildfire. Everything outside the bubble was complicated, impossible, but right now, at this moment, breathing in his masculine scent and feeling his warm breath against her face, she could imagine what being with him would be like. If she was with him, even for a little while, perhaps she'd know peace, joy, love...

Tears clung to her lashes. Those dreaded emotions were bubbling back up inside her, and she couldn't bury them, not when he was this close. It frayed her control and made her nerves raw.

"I can't do that, Carter. I'm not..." She sucked in a sob. "I have to do what's best for Matthew. Someone has to, and you know my parents. I just want—" She wiped at her eyes, hating how much keeping the truth from him hurt.

"Celia—"

"I want to be with you," she finally admitted, her soul soaring the moment she allowed herself to savor that truth. She saw the growing pleasure and hope in his eyes, and she amended, "I want to be with you— for a little while. Before it has to end."

Pain filled his eyes, but he didn't argue with her. Instead, he nodded in understanding. He'd always understood her. It was one of the things that made this man so bloody perfect, so dangerously wonderful.

"Tell me what you want me to do," he whispered as she sidled a step closer. His scent enveloped her again, drugging her with its comforting aroma. There was a hint of leather and sandalwood. She wished she could bottle it up and keep it with her forever.

She tilted her chin up. He gazed at her with eyes that promised her the world if she only asked. How could he do that? Be so perfect?

"Callum and I agreed that we need time before we

make the announcement official. He misses Bryson, and I told my mother I'm going to visit Aunt Holly for a month. She lives in Tuscany during the summer. I was hoping... Would you come with me?"

Celia reached for his hands and clasped them in her own. They were always afraid to touch in public because there was usually someone watching her. But not now, not here in the servants' quarters. A hundred years ago she would have feared being discovered with Carter and shamed by her association with a servant. It seemed times hadn't changed much. There was still an expectation that men and women didn't break the barriers of upstairs and downstairs.

He exhaled slowly, and she prayed he wouldn't say no. "Celia, your father would never—"

She pressed a fingertip to his lips, silencing him. "He won't know. Please, Carter."

It was her dream, ever since she'd been a little girl. Her prince charming wasn't a man with a title or a vast estate. He was just the man who loved her. This would be their last chance. Their *only* chance. He had to say yes.

"Please, if we can't have anything else, give me this."

He lowered his head and pressed his lips to hers. He kissed her slowly, sweetly, as though he was trying to hold back his hunger, but she could taste it on his lips. She couldn't help but smile a little, even though her face was wet with tears.

"Everything is going to be all right," he murmured against her lips. "I promise."

It had been so long since she'd come alive when she kissed someone. Hell, if she was honest, no one had ever kissed her like Carter had. A whisper of a thrill danced at the edges of her fingertips. She shivered in his arms, nervous and frightened, but she kept smiling. They hadn't kissed since they were fourteen. So much had changed, and it was as though he was discovering her lips all over again. The kiss scorched her, reminded her what her heart and body had always whispered whenever he was near. That he was the only man for her.

As a teen, she'd often imagined herself like the fabled Guinevere and Carter as her Lancelot. Drawn together by love but kept apart by honor and duty. Now more than ever she felt that wild desperation, like the ill-fated queen, to have her moment with him before she accepted her fate.

When they broke apart, he stroked her cheeks with the pads of his thumbs. She clasped his wrists with her hands, clinging to him.

"When do we leave?" he asked.

Celia bit her lip, then replied, "Tomorrow."

A shadow passed across his face.

"What's the matter?"

"It's my father. I've taken over half of his duties running the Pembroke estate. He has so much to take care of. If I leave him for that long..." He closed his eyes for a brief moment. He rarely talked about his work, but Celia knew it was important to him. He helped keep the lands running, the manor house repaired, the taxes paid, the accounts balanced, and the work was almost always thankless. She knew he had other dreams, ones he kept hidden from the world. If only he could have been brave enough to share them with her...

"Tell Tristan, but no one else. He can help us. I know it." She cupped his face and stood up on her tiptoes to feather her lips over his again.

The kiss, although light, sent bolts of hunger through her. He grasped her waist, dragging her to him as he deepened the kiss. Their passion sent her head spinning like she'd had too much brandy. When they finally broke apart, she was breathless and held a hand to her kiss-swollen lips.

Carter glanced out the window to where her

cousin and Kat were still dancing. "You're right. He will help us." Tristan knew more than anyone else what it was like to love someone forbidden to him.

"I have to go," Celia said, looking around. "I'll meet you at the airport tomorrow morning. I'll text you the flight information." She squeezed his hand one more time, even though she ached to kiss him again. His eyes told her what she already knew. If they kissed again now, they might not be able to stop.

"See you soon."

She bit her lip, still smiling, and slipped out the servants' door and into the light to face the crowds.

Tomorrow she'd fly to Italy with Carter. For one month it would be just the two of them. She ignored the knot of tension in her chest at the thought of what would happen afterward. All that mattered now was that she had bought them a brief time in paradise, and she wasn't going to allow herself to have any regrets.

❧ 2 ❧

Tristan Kingsley gaped at Carter in shock. "You're going to do *what?*"

Carter grumbled and took a large drink from his pint. "You heard." They were sharing a drink in the local pub in Haresbury, a little town not too far from the Pembroke estate just outside London.

"It's reckless, foolish, and likely to get you shot. I approve." Tristan's blue-green eyes sparkled with mischief. "You and Celia in Italy for an entire month? Tell me you won't spend the entire time mooning at her with calf-eyes and begging to hold her hand. I'd hoped you'd be well past that by now."

Carter frowned. "You're encouraging me to shag your cousin?"

Tristan frowned. "Well...er...put it like that and it doesn't sound good. Make love to her sounds better. Actually, saying nothing at all sounds better—we both know what we're talking about. Point is, you'd better not waste a damned moment. I made that mistake with Kat, and it almost cost me my life." Tristan pointed to a faint scar near his left temple, a reminder of Tristan's nearly fatal car accident the previous winter. He'd been run off the road by a paparazzi SUV while trying to drive from London to Cambridge to see Kat.

"I don't plan on wasting any time, but I can't just jump her bones the moment we land, now can I?"

Tristan smirked. "Why not before? I quite enjoyed joining the mile-high club, as the Americans call it. Of course, you'd have to be on the same plane for that to happen, and knowing you, you'll fly economy while she takes my father's jet."

Carter rolled his eyes. "Yes, well, we have to have some discretion in all this." His best friend had been a notorious womanizer until he'd met Kat. Fortunately, she had changed him for the better. "And yes, she's taking your father's jet. I'm flying economy."

"A sad statement in and of itself. Oh well, another time then." Tristan seemed undeterred. "Just don't hold back, that's all I'm saying. For once in your bloody life, you'll get to be with the woman you're crazy about. Seize the moment."

If only it were that easy. But he had spent so long denying his hunger and love for Celia. "I don't even know what to do," he admitted.

Tristan wagged a finger at him. "I seem to recall more than one night where you didn't go home alone. You've spent the last seven years bedding women as though your life depended on it. Surely you know how to woo a woman into your bedroom, especially one who wants you. How hard can it be?"

His past relationships weren't something he was proud of. But Tristan was right—he'd done his damnedest to forget Celia, at least for a few hours while he was with someone else. Sometimes the physical release worked, but only for the briefest moments. In the end, he saw only one woman in his mind, and his lips formed only one name.

"I still can't believe you're going to do it. I *especially* can't believe it was Celia's idea." Tristan shook his head and finished his pint.

Carter swirled his own glass, staring at the amber liquid that made him think of Celia's hazel eyes and how he wished he was already headed for Italy. Celia was the sort of girl who always did the right thing, even to her own detriment. Protecting her little brother had always been a priority for her. It was one of many things he loved about her. But at the same time, it kept them apart. She would always put her brother first before herself.

And I have no way to help her. There was no way he could raise the funds necessary to put Matthew through school at Ravenswood. If he had another year or two, maybe, but...

"And to think she's marrying Callum," Tristan added, snapping him out of his thoughts. "Nice fellow and all, for an Oxford man. But what about Bryson? I know his parents don't know and wouldn't approve, but this is the twenty-first century, for God's sake. Pity. Bryson's a good man."

"Yes, Celia and Callum are both doing what they believe is a duty to their families. He's giving his family an heir, and she's making sure Matthew will be cared for."

"If it were any more tragic, you'd think Shake-speare would have written it," Tristan mused. "Father's still furious that they invested their money so poorly, you know. Uncle Hensley's a damned fool. Father had to call in a lot of favors to save them. A lot of the estate's cash has been used to pay their debts."

"I know," said Carter. It was part of the reason the two of them were collaborating on a little side project for the estate. One they hoped would pay dividends.

"It's made for a tense couple of months, I can tell you. I was glad to loan Celia my flat in London so she doesn't have to stay in that tiny cottage with her parents all the time. They'd likely kill each other after a month of living together. I only wish I could have helped more." Tristan shook his head and sighed.

"I wish I had a way to give her what she needs," Carter said, half to himself. But he had barely a thousand pounds to his name. Being a junior steward wasn't about being rich—it was about having a position that mattered and loving what you did.

Tristan placed a palm on his shoulder. "Don't hit me for suggesting this, but have you talked about... after the marriage? About still seeing each other?"

Carter shook his head. "Her marriage to Callum might be a marriage of convenience, but I won't be the other man, and she wouldn't want me to be. Besides, what happens when a child becomes involved? No, it's not who we are."

"So much for the twenty-first century," Tristan replied. "You always were the better of the two of us. I got good looks and pragmatism, and you got honor."

They chuckled, and then Tristan turned serious again. "Don't give up. We still have time. I've made more calls to producers in Los Angeles. It might pay off."

"Right." Carter tried to smile. He and Tristan and been working for more than a year to get Hollywood interested in the estate for filming period pieces. The payout could be huge, but only if the producers felt it had the location qualities they were looking for.

"Carter, have faith. Celia isn't destined to marry Callum. She's always been yours. You know that. Don't stop believing it, even for a second."

She loves me, I know she does. The thought filled his chest with a silly warmth that he couldn't contain. But it was tempered with the cold reality that he couldn't provide for her, let alone Matthew.

Carter downed the last of his pint as well. They both stood and slapped a few extra pounds on the table before they left. It would be a nice walk this evening back to the estate, one he could use to clear his head. The town of Haresbury was little more than a few cobblestoned streets of tiny cottages with moss-covered roofs and window boxes overwhelmed with flowers. The perfume of the blooms in late May were heady and intoxicating. It blessed a man with sweet dreams at night, dreams of holding and kissing the woman he loved for hours on end.

He'd fantasized more than once of how he would take Celia picnicking and lay her back on the blanket and drink of her lips like wine and taste strawberries upon her skin. She would be a glorious feast, and he'd savor every minute of it.

As a child, he'd run through the fields of the Pembroke estate with her, watching her stain her dresses with grass and get her hands dirty as she climbed trees with him and Tristan, but that had changed when he and Tristan had left for Eton. Carter had been fortunate enough that her uncle had paid for him to attend a school usually reserved for the sons of the British elite. Celia's parents had separated her from her cousin, sending her to an all-girl's school since Eton was for boys only. She'd come back polished like any young lady of good breeding. It was only when she looked at him that he saw the hint of her old wildness hiding behind her eyes, the days of forests and childhood laughter like warm sunlight on her face, filling his heart with heat and light.

He was still smiling as he and Tristan walked up the steps to Pembroke's manor house. They met one of the footmen at the door, a young man named Eddie.

"Late night, eh?" Eddie chuckled, nodding in deference to Tristan. Tristan slapped Eddie on the shoulder and laughed.

"Going to be even later for this one. He has to pack for a trip and have a talk with his father. It's a toss-up as to which will take longer." Tristan smirked as he left Carter and Eddie standing in the entry hall.

Eddie nodded at Tristan's back as he climbed the stairs to go to his room, tripping on the last step. "What was that all about?"

"It's the ale talking," said Carter. "But I do need to speak to my father. Do you know where he is?" Carter wasn't about to tell Eddie he was running off to Italy with Celia. He trusted Eddie, but old houses had big ears, and the last thing he needed was for his clandestine plans to become public knowledge. He'd never make it to the airport. Celia's father would likely have him shot and buried in the woods.

"Last I saw, he was in his office."

"Still working?" Carter didn't like the sound of that. His father had been working too hard of late, and it was taking a toll on him. Running a vast estate was complicated and stressful, and it wasn't easy, even for John Martin, to please Lord Pembroke. That was why Carter had been taking over more of his father's duties lately.

Things would be different when Tristan was in charge. Unlike Edward Kingsley, Tristan was more relaxed in his control and expectations, but he also had a great deal of vision when it came to Pembroke's future. And Carter would be there at his side, helping the estate survive into the future. So many other estates had been broken up and sold to the highest bidders. Carter and Tristan had vowed to never let that happen. It was their destiny to keep Pembroke intact.

But destiny was a funny thing. It had drawn him and Tristan together like two magnets, while it kept him and Celia oceans apart.

Carter walked down the corridor to his father's office in the servants' area, which was between the butler's office, and the housekeeper's. Carter saw the light on and walked in without knocking.

John Martin was seated at his mahogany desk, buried in papers. He glanced up, squinting, and floundered for his glasses. Carter stepped closer and nudged the glasses into his father's searching fingers.

"Ah, Carter," he sighed, but there was a smile on his lips. "You and Tristan back from the pub?"

"Yes." Carter wondered if that would earn him a reprimand. His father usually frowned on any activities that kept either him or the future earl from tending to their duties.

Martin chuckled. "Can't say I blame you. Today's party was quite exhausting. Mr. Langley's only just sent the servants to bed after cleaning up. Thank God the caterers were able to help put away tables afterward. I certainly don't want to see the champagne bill."

"Father," Carter began.

His father was back to looking at his papers again. "Yes?" He pushed his glasses down his nose so he could peer over the top.

"I'm leaving for Italy tomorrow. I'll be gone a month. I've spoken to Tristan; he's going to help you with the accounts and the running of the grounds while I'm away."

Martin nudged his glasses back up his nose and set his papers down.

"Italy?" The word implied a thousand questions, but as always, his father was patient with him.

"Er, yes. Celia's invited me. I'm going to go with her while she visits her aunt in Tuscany."

Martin's eyes widened. "You and Miss Lynton?"

Carter nodded. "Yes."

This was something they'd never spoken of. His love for Celia was a thing that more often than not hurt him, and his father was the sort of man to never harm his son if he could manage it.

"I trust you are aware of her engagement to Lord Cavanaugh's son? I know it isn't public knowledge, but it occurred today during the party." His father always managed to know everything that occurred on the Pembroke estate.

"I'm quite aware. I also know it's a marriage of convenience. They've both agreed to take one month of...freedom before going public with their engagement." He felt like a boy caught stealing tarts from the kitchen, but he didn't know how else to explain it to his father. This was his one chance to be with Celia before life forced them apart.

His father sighed again, the sound far heavier this time. "And afterward?"

Carter shook his head. His father grunted and nodded. "I see."

He wasn't fool enough to believe that he'd ever be with Celia, not in the way he wished, but perhaps a month could last a lifetime in his memory. And it didn't stop him from hoping that he and Tristan might have success in getting some producers to look at Pembroke for a filming location. If they could manage it before the month was up, maybe it could save everything. Lord Pembroke had graciously agreed that if Carter managed to get the estate used for filming, he'd receive ten percent of the payment for the estate's use. If a studio offered enough, with his small percentage he could ask Celia to marry him instead, and he could cover Matthew's tuition. There would be the wrath of her parents and Lord Pembroke, of course. But he'd risk all of it for her. And he believed she would do the same.

But time was the enemy. Matthew would start school in two months, and no miracle was in sight.

His father studied him, missing nothing. "As long as you check with his lordship and have him approve the holiday, then I will allow it."

"Thank you, Father. Where is Lord Pembroke?"

"The evening room, I believe, having a much-needed drink."

Carter slipped out of his father's office and headed for the evening room. The house was quiet. No doubt Tristan was already curled up around Kat in their bedroom. On any other night he would have been lonely, but with the promise of seeing Celia tomorrow, and for the next month, he had no room in his heart for loneliness.

He found Edward, Lord Pembroke, reclining in a chair by the fire, an old leather-bound book in one hand and a glass of brandy in the other. Carter rapped his knuckles on the open door, and Pembroke looked up.

"Ah, Carter, come in." He set his book down and gestured to an empty chair by the fire.

It was perhaps unusual for a steward's son to sit in the presence of an earl with such familiarity, but Lord Pembroke had always had a soft spot for him—not that Carter had the faintest clue why. The man was usually a devil to deal with, even with regard to how he treated his own son.

Carter stood next to the chair but didn't sit. "My apologies, my lord, for disturbing you. I've spoken to my father, and having received his approval for a vacation, I now seek yours."

Pembroke straightened in his chair. "Oh?"

"Er...yes. I've been invited to spend a month in Italy, starting tomorrow. I have enough saved up to pay for lodging and expenses."

The earl's eyes brightened. "And who has invited you?"

Carter held his breath before replying, knowing it could possibly get him fired. "Miss Lynton is the one who extended the invitation."

Pembroke raised a brow. "My niece? Are Tristan and Kat going with you?"

"No."

"Hmm." The earl made a soft sound and then chuckled. "Let me guess—you've taken a page out of my son's book? Going to start a wildfire of rumors in London by running off with a young lady who's engaged herself to a future earl?"

"We aren't running off. We're just..." He didn't

know the words, couldn't seem to find a way to explain his plans.

"Not running off?" Pembroke watched him as intently as his father had.

"She needs some time before she and Radcliffe..." He didn't want to finish the thought or picture that future date. It would only crush the happiness he would have for the next month.

"You are so like your mother," Pembroke said.

"My mother?" He knew that his mother had lived on the estate before she'd married his father, but he hadn't thought she'd crossed paths with the earl much, if at all.

"Yes, she was all fire and spirit, not afraid to follow her heart, much like yourself. You know full well that my niece will marry the Radcliffe boy, but you'll spend what time you can with her. That's it, isn't it?"

Carter stared into the fire, watching the flames, unable to meet Pembroke's gaze.

"If it's one hour or a month, it doesn't matter. I will take however long she will give me." He tensed when the earl stood and placed a hand on his shoulder.

"You have your mother's gray eyes too. I miss her very much. She brought so much life to this house." The man smiled as though remembering something from long ago, then became serious again. "Very well, you have my permission. Go on now."

"Thank you, my lord." Carter exited the room, a strange tightness in his chest. The earl knew the color of his mother's eyes?

He stood in the corridor for a moment, and his cell phone vibrated. He pulled it out of his pocket and saw it was a text from Celia.

Hope you're packing. Bring your swim trunks. Aunt Holly has a pool.

For a moment he made himself forget that this

was going to be his only chance for her to be his. He wanted to believe this was the beginning of something, not the beginning of the end. A smile crept across his lips and soon took over his whole face as he typed a response.

When we go swimming, we won't need suits.

She didn't respond, but rather than be upset, he started to laugh. No doubt she'd been embarrassed by that. It was going to be a fun month. Celia had become too proper, but while they were in Italy, he was going to show her how wonderful being bad with him could be.

❦ 3 ❦

I shouldn't be this nervous. There is no reason to be freaking out.

Celia shot a glance at Carter as their private car pulled onto the long dirt road that led to her aunt's villa just outside Siena. She continued to sneak glances at him, glad her sunglasses could hide her checking him out. He looked so damned good in his jeans and black T-shirt. He wore a pair of aviators, and his blond hair was slightly windswept as he stared out the car window. A shadow of dark-gold stubble glittered like gold dust in the late-evening sun.

She swallowed, her mouth a little dry as she noticed for the tenth time that she could see his T-shirt clinging to his abs. It was rare for her to see him dressed so casually. They had never been truly alone together since they were children, except for the drive from London to Cambridge the previous winter after Tristan's car crash. But there had been no enjoying that moment then because they'd been so worried.

Now they were here in Italy, just the two of them, and for the first time in her life she was nervous. Because she knew what might...what she *wanted* to have happen between them. She wanted one last taste of freedom, and she wanted to spend that time with the only man she'd ever loved.

Carter turned away from the window. "How is it that I've never met your aunt before?" He reached across the seat between them and took her hand in his, setting it on his lap so he could stroke the back of her hand with his fingertips. The move felt so natural, as though he'd always caressed it like that.

She had trouble thinking past the delighted hum his touch created in her head, like lazy summer bees outside their hives. It made her want to lie down in the grass and soak up the sun and the euphoria of it all.

"She's my father's younger sister, but they've never gotten along. She doesn't come home much anymore. They only end up fighting." She watched his elegant fingers trace mysterious patterns on her hand.

"Is she a free spirit? That seems like the sort of thing he'd object to."

He still brushed his fingers over her skin, and it gave her delicious goosebumps on her arms.

"You could say that. She's never wanted the life my grandparents laid out for her. They wanted her to marry up in the aristocracy, be the wife of a peer."

"The usual," Carter added flatly.

"But she had other ideas. She came here to study painting, fell in love with this country and a man she met here, Stefano. He died only a few years ago. He's the one who left her the villa."

She looked at the villa through the windows ahead, the rolling green landscape dotted with cypress trees in long lines. It was an old stone villa. The gardens that led up to the house were lush, with bushes trimmed in perfect geometrical shapes. Fountains were covered in lily pads, the white stone statues gleaming in the sun.

Carter exhaled as he leaned forward to get a better look. "My God."

She understood his reaction. There was nothing more spectacular than an English countryside estate, but an Italian villa was…an entirely different and magical experience. It felt warm and enticing in a way those in England never could. It was as though the winter never came here. No blizzards could touch the glowing hills with their waving gold grass and dark-green trees that stretched into the sky.

Celia tried to hide a smile as the car stopped in front of the house. Her aunt was standing in the doorway, holding an orange striped cat with one arm and waving at them with the other. Holly was a willowy forty-year-old woman, but she still looked like she was in her early thirties. She might have even been able to pass for Celia's older sister. She wore a pale-pink sundress and cork wedge sandals, fitting right in with the sunny Italian landscape.

"Celia!" Holly set the cat down on the ground and opened the car door for her. Celia had to pull her hand from Carter's grip as she got out. He exited from his side of the vehicle and paid the driver his tip before turning to the boot of the car to fetch the luggage.

"Well, hello there, handsome," Holly breathed as she stared at Carter's lean, muscled form. Holly offered her hand to Carter as he reached her. "I'm Holly Rossi."

"Carter Martin. Pleasure."

"Oh, the pleasure is *all* mine," she said with a predatory smile. Carter shook her hand before he retrieved their suitcases from the trunk and followed behind them as they walked inside the house.

"Holly, you're terrible!" Celia nudged her aunt with an elbow.

Holly looped her arm through Celia's and leaned in to whisper, "I may be a widow, but that doesn't mean I can't appreciate a gorgeous man. Does that make me a cougar?" Holly beamed mischievously at her niece.

"Only if you try to steal him. He's mine," she declared with pride and no small amount of possessiveness. At least, he was for now.

"I see..." Holly sobered. "Your father doesn't know about this young man, does he?"

Celia glanced over her shoulder to make sure Carter hadn't come in yet, then shook her head.

"Father would kill me if he found out. I suppose you know about my engagement to Callum?"

"Yes, and I take it that engagement is not what it appears to be?"

Celia nodded. "When we have a minute alone, I'll explain." She only hoped her aunt would understand.

"I'm sure you will, but I think I can take a guess. We'll talk later then," Holly said. Her hazel eyes gleamed with an understanding that only a woman who had defied Celia's father could have. "You two will have a wonderful time here. I'll make sure of it."

As Carter entered, he smiled at her, and it hit her right behind the knees, just like it had for the last nineteen years.

Yes, we will have a wonderful time here.

"Let's get you settled in your room er...rooms." Holly winked at them. "Then you two can relax by the pool before dinner. We'll eat around eight."

Holly's villa was a mixture of various old-world architecture and designs, with vaulted ceilings and stones of roughhewn rock mixed with warm buttery yellow painted walls. Paintings dotted the spaces between the rooms, a parade of faces that were sometimes solemn, sometimes full of life. Celia knew her aunt was a lover of the arts, and her home reflected that.

"We can put Carter here." They stopped in front of a room on the left side of the hall, and Carter carried his suitcase inside. Holly nodded at a door across the hall. "And, Celia, you're over here."

Celia bit her lip. She had no intention of sleeping in a different room than Carter, but she could at least leave her things there. Celia picked up her valise and carried it into the room. It had a beautiful queen-size bed with a wrought-iron canopy that looked warm and inviting.

"I'll leave you two to settle in. Just come down to the pool whenever you're ready."

"Thanks, Holly." Celia hugged her aunt, loving that she was so open and caring, unlike her parents. She could never understand how she and Matthew had come from that union. Her parents were schemers, social climbers, and snobbish. At times, she was filled with rage that they were so focused on society, wouldn't do their real jobs, wouldn't take care of their child. No, they made *her* be the parent, the responsible one, made *her* be the one to sacrifice her happiness to take care of him.

Well, at least now she had a month to be selfish, to have the one thing she'd ever wanted in life. The one person.

Celia abandoned her suitcase and crossed the hall, stopping in the doorway to Carter's room. He'd removed his sunglasses and was setting his suitcase on his bed. The lean lines of his tall legs in his jeans made her want to press up against him from behind and just *purr*. But wanting and doing were two different things. Aside from the one kiss they'd shared at the party and a stolen kiss at fourteen, they hadn't been intimate in any way. It was nerve-racking. How did a girl handle wanting to jump a man's bones when they'd known each other all their lives but had only kissed twice?

She walked up quietly behind him and was about to touch his shoulder when he spun, catching her by the waist, grinning.

"Never could sneak up on me, you know," he teased. His eyes had brightened to an iridescent silvery blue-gray.

She trailed her fingertips along his jaw. For a man without noble ancestry, his face was a thing of aristocratic beauty. He was cut from marble, a sculptor's dream.

His hands spanned her waist, and she was all too aware she wore only a dress, a simple short-skirted rose dress with a black belt that he could easily push up to her hips. Her knees buckled at the thought.

"Whoa there," he whispered, catching her as she fell more heavily against him.

"Sorry." She ducked her head shyly. He was the only man she'd ever met who could make her weak at the knees like that. She'd once had dinner with Prince William and Prince Harry at the peak of their bachelorhood, and she hadn't been flustered in the slightest, despite how charming they had been. Yet without trying, Carter made her feel like a lovesick teenage girl.

"How's your room?" He gently pushed her back, the distance a declaration that he wasn't ready yet—or perhaps he was just giving her time. Either way, her body burned with frustration at the separation. He focused on the luggage, turning away from her.

"Fine, but I was thinking that we don't really *need* two rooms."

Carter had been opening his suitcase, his back partially to her when she said this. His hands lingered on the suitcase snaps before he turned his head toward her, glancing at her out of the corner of his eye.

"We don't need two rooms?" Carter echoed.

It felt as though they were dancing an old dance, one from a hundred years before their time, where they dared to slide a step too close, their hands lingering, their faces shining, before they had to swirl apart and turn away. They were dancing around the very reason she'd brought him here, and she was afraid to ask for what she wanted from him outright.

"I thought..." She swallowed hard, fighting for breath. Why did this make her so bloody nervous?

"Celia, I know I agreed to come here with you, but before anything happens, I have to be clear. I don't want to be *that* man. I know your marriage to Callum will be in name only, but what happens here, this month, that's all I can give you. We can't risk anything else. It could ruin your uncle's reputation and the estate, and it could wreck Callum's relationship with his parents."

Celia's heart froze. "I know. But I need time to make memories that I can carry with me." Once married, she and Callum would focus on the child he needed and giving that child a happy life, no matter the cost. But this moment right now was her only chance to have a glimpse of true happiness.

"If there was a way you could be with me...if...I could help with Matthew...if I..." He seemed to struggle with the words, and she understood.

"I wish no one had to help me with Matthew. I wish I could afford the tuition myself. And I wish more than anything that you and I..." She couldn't finish either.

Carter's hands dropped from the suitcase to his sides as he turned to face her. He nodded his understanding, then turned back to his suitcase and pulled out a pair of swim trunks.

"I need to change," he said softly. When he didn't meet her eyes, she managed a weak smile and fled back to her room. She closed the door and leaned back against it, her blood pounding in her ears and her heart aching with sharp pain.

How stupid she was to think this would be perfect. That they could pretend that Callum, the engagement, and her parents never existed.

So much for my last chance at love.

❧ 4 ❧

Carter stared at the contents of his suitcase, his heart pounding. He was really here with Celia in Italy. For the entire flight he had been in a kind of daze. But now he was here in a lavish Italian bedroom in a multimillion-dollar villa. His blood hummed in his veins, all because Celia was across the hall and nothing stood between them.

I could go to her room right now and... He stopped that train of thought before it rocketed into dangerous territory. He wasn't some randy teenager. If he couldn't control his hormones or his lust, he would scare Celia. Not to mention he'd just put the brakes on their relationship seconds ago by reminding her that this thing between them wouldn't last. Not his finest moment. He'd have to fix that, give her the happiness he'd promised while they were here.

He raked a hand through his hair and closed his eyes as he centered himself. A swim would clear his head. He removed his jeans and boots, put on his trunks and sunglasses, and headed into the hall. Celia's bedroom door was closed. He guessed she still needed a few more minutes. That was fine. He wanted to get the lay of the land anyway. He'd lived on a big estate his whole life, so he'd learned to familiarize himself with a house's layout in case he ever needed to know where something was. But now he was supposed to be relaxing and enjoying himself.

You are not the help here. You are a guest.

The voice in the back of his head was right, but he couldn't shake the urge to get to know all the rooms. But that would have to wait. He wandered back down the hall until he reached the main living room, which had wide open terrace doors that led out to the pool. Carter whistled in appreciation. A long infinity pool stretched along the deck. Beyond it was a scenic view of rolling green-and-gold hills, lit by warm sunlight that painted the world in blazing hues of rich color. The water was a brilliant blue as it reflected the sky.

Holly joined him when he took a step onto the weathered stone deck. "You like it?"

The deck was warm beneath his bare feet, but not too hot. Celia's aunt was trying to hide a mischievous smile. Carter couldn't help but think Celia might have been like her, all wild, delightfully rebellious, if she hadn't gone to a finishing school and spent much of her free time watching over Matthew her whole life. Matthew was a great kid, but that didn't erase the sorrow Carter felt when he thought of Celia sacrificing her own happiness for him. That selflessness was one of the many reasons he loved her. He knew he was a lucky bastard to have this one month with her. He had to make the most of it.

"This place... It's..." Carter struggled for words. Holly chuckled.

"I know. Stefano had fantastic taste in architecture." Her smile slipped a little. She shrugged off her grief and nodded toward a row of deck chairs.

"Grab a towel and a chair. I'll make us some drinks." She walked over to a fancy outdoor bar in the pool house at the far end. Carter retrieved a towel from a stack by the terrace doors and headed to the nearest deck chair. He stripped off his shirt and tossed it across the back of his chair and waded onto the top steps of the pool. Once he was waist deep, he plunged beneath the surface and swam a few yards before coming back up. He flicked his hair out of his eyes and noticed someone moving at the open doorway.

Celia stood there, watching him. He noted the red bikini she wore, with a light see-through knit cover-up top that came halfway down her thighs. She wore the cutest pair of wedge sandals with red straps. Was she thinking about him the way he was thinking about her right now? He got hard just imagining those sandals digging into his shoulders while he—

Carter snapped his control back into place as Celia stepped out into the sunlight. Her blonde hair came down past her shoulders in loose waves, like a blonde haired heroine from a Titian painting, and her eyes locked on his as she set her towel down on the chair next to his. She turned her back on him as she slid her feet out of the sandals and lifted her cover off. Carter's eyes were drawn to her heart-shaped bottom and that little red swimsuit. Completely mesmerized, he leaned against the side of the pool and waited for her to turn around.

When she did, her face was flushed. She rushed to the shallow edge of the pool and ducked into the water. Carter bit the inside of his cheek to hide a grin. Celia had always been modest, shy even. He had never seen her wear anything so revealing before, and clearly she wasn't used to it. Then he sobered. Was she wearing a sexy bikini because she felt desperate? The thought left a sour taste in his mouth. He didn't want Celia to feel that way, and yet he feared she did. She'd agreed to marry Callum because he was the safest way to assure Matthew got into Ravenswood. Now she was here, spending her last free month with him.

It was the very definition of desperate.

Carter leaned back, reached for the sunglasses he'd left at the side of the pool, and put them on. The aviators hid his eyes, and he was grateful for the shield. He didn't want Celia to see his own doubts and worries. He always felt like an open book whenever she looked at him.

She began to swim, performing a perfect breaststroke, coming up wet, her hair slicked back. Drops of water still clung to her dark-gold lashes as she joined him at the side of the pool.

"It's so beautiful," she said with a little weary sigh. His heart ached. God, she was amazing, smart, and selfless. She was carrying the weight of her entire family on her shoulders.

Carter's throat tightened. "Gorgeous countryside. Your aunt is lucky."

"She is, but she misses Stefano. He was a great guy. I had the fortune of meeting him two years ago when they visited London." Celia leaned against the pool's edge next to him, her shoulder almost touching his, but her eyes were looking toward her aunt and the pool house. Holly brought them two mixed drinks, and then with a wink, she headed back into the house.

"I thought Aunt Holly might stay...," Celia began.

He chuckled. "I think your aunt is giving us some time alone."

Carter tested the drink, vodka, cranberry juice, and a twist of lime. Not bad.

"Well, she's awfully sweet. I'll owe her a dozen favors after this. I can't believe we're actually here." Celia giggled and took a big gulp of her drink. Bigger than he'd expected.

"Steady on." Carter slipped her glass from her hand and set it on the side of the pool.

She frowned at him. "Hey, I wanted to finish that." She crossed her arms over her chest, which only accented the tantalizing view of her breasts in that red bikini top.

"We have all afternoon and tonight," he said as he leaned in and cupped her cheek.

Her lashes lowered. "Carter..." When she said his name that way, full of uncertainty, he understood. This was too fast, and he didn't want to push her. He only wanted her to be happy.

"Hey, it's okay." He pulled her into his arms in a hug. She sighed, relaxing into him, her cheek pressed against his chest. "You call the shots."

"I'm sorry. It's just... I'm so nervous," she whispered. "Can we take it slow?"

He tilted her face up with his fingertips. "We can take it as slow as you want. I'm here for you. Whatever you want, just ask." He'd take it slow, even if it killed him.

Her lips curved in a teasing grin. "My very own Carter toy, eh?" She brushed a kiss on his cheek and then dove back into the water, swimming away from him. Carter let her go, grinning to himself. Her very own Carter toy? Oh, he would let her play with him *any* way she wanted.

She swam a few laps, and he finished his drink as he watched her. Then she fetched two pool mats from the pool house and handed him one. They both climbed on the mats, drifting in quiet silence on the surface of the water. Carter tried to relax and let the sun soak into him.

This was a real vacation, something he hadn't had in years. Being the steward of a large English estate could be very stressful. They needed a third person to help them, but recent cutbacks had done away with that possibility. However, if Carter and Tristan's plan to get film producers interested in the estate was successful, they might even be able to hire two.

He tried to ignore the twinge of guilt he felt at leaving his father alone. But Tristan had assured

Carter that he would help however he could while he was gone.

Carter wasn't sure how long he dozed before he realized he and Celia had drifted closer. Her hand reached out and grasped his, and he linked their fingers together in the water. A smile twisted the corners of her lips, though her eyes remained closed.

"Tristan said you got your job at Morton & Ridings," he said quietly, half afraid he would disturb her peace. "Congratulations."

"Thanks." She didn't open her eyes, so he had a moment to burn the stunning image of her profile deep into his heart. She was a classic beauty, but he'd been with beauties before. What made Celia special was not her pale-pink lips or hazel eyes—it was the way she acted, the things she said and even the way she touched him, as she did now. The entire world seemed to fall away, leaving just the two of them.

He'd spent his entire life feeling less than suitable for a woman like Celia in every possible way. Not handsome enough, educated enough, rich enough, or powerful enough. But whenever he was with her he felt like was more of everything he wanted to be.

"Are you excited?" he asked. She had wanted to be an architect for a long time. Getting her degree had been a struggle because her parents had fought her progress every step of the way.

"I am, but it doesn't pay as well as I'd hoped. Not yet. But I think they genuinely like my designs."

Carter tightened his hold on her hand. "You've never shown me any of your work. Could I see it?"

Celia opened her eyes and turned her head in his direction. "You really want to?" The shock in her gaze hurt him. She had so little confidence at times. Her parents had done too good of a job convincing her that she had no talent. He'd grown up watching her suffer from the emotional neglect and sometimes even emotional abuse they'd dealt. Luckily, Matthew was in his own world so often he didn't seem to register that he was a disappointment to them. But Celia was all too aware of how she'd disappointed her parents. She'd suffered the slings and arrows for both of them.

"I'd love it more than anything," he assured her. "Let's get dried off, and you can show me some designs."

He slipped off his mat and climbed out of the pool, retrieving a couple of towels. She met him at the shallow end and took one from him, wrapping it around her body.

Holly stepped out onto the deck, noticing they were coming inside. "Are either of you hungry? Dinner's about ready"

"That would be great." The designs would have to wait. Celia would likely want to shower before dinner, and he ought to as well. They finished drying off and returned to their rooms. He watched Celia's bottom sway, even through the large towel, and he released a slow breath before he entered his own room. His shower was going to be ice-cold.

Celia spent her entire time in the shower fantasizing about Carter. She still couldn't believe she was here with him, and yet she was hesitant about everything. She wanted him like crazy, but she was afraid. Not of him, but of what happened next. What if she learned she couldn't live without him? What if she decided to abandon everything she'd arranged, just for him? She would lose everything, and Matthew's future would be in jeopardy.

But the idea of living a life without knowing love, if only for a little while, was just as unbearable. She couldn't resist him, not for long, not in this sunny, seductive place so far from home. She didn't *want* to resist him. It was why she'd come here, after all.

"Stop being so silly," she told her reflection in the bathroom mirror. She could do this. She could spend the month in Carter's arms, and then she could go on with her life for Matthew's sake. She had to.

She splashed some water on her hands in the sink and pressed them against her face. The cold water woke up her senses. She dried her face and brushed her hair back, then plucked a few bobby pins out of her accessories case and pinned the locks back. The effect was a loose tumble of blonde waves pulled back to leave her face exposed.

With a nod of satisfaction, she retrieved an emerald-green knee-length dress she'd packed and slipped it on. A deep green like this would make her hazel eyes appear more green than brown. She enjoyed dressing up, and now more than ever it seemed to be vital that she looked her best for Carter. She was quite sure Carter would want her even if she wore a dress made from a burlap sack. But she wanted their time here together to be perfect, and she wanted to feel beautiful with him. She donned a pair of gold gladiator strappy sandals to complete the look and exited the bedroom.

The distant sounds of music lured her to the outside patio opposite the pool. Glittering strings of lights hung from the wooden beams that formed the patio's ceiling. A table that could seat six people had been set for three. Her aunt carryied out a large bowl of salad.

Carter was crouched in front of an old record player, flipping through a box of vinyl records. He looked positively mouthwatering in his tight jeans and navy-blue polo shirt.

"Stefano had fantastic taste in music, Holly." Carter stood, an album in his hands, and placed the record on the turntable. A song from the fifties or maybe the sixties came on, and Carter snapped his fingers to the beat. When he turned around and finally saw her, his hands dropped to his sides. He gazed at her, and her knees threatened to buckle, like they so often did around him. He looked at her like she was the last woman on earth and held the key to his salvation. And she knew, without a doubt, that her face mirrored the hunger and need she felt.

"Celia, you look..." He bit his lip, uncertain of what to say next. Holly nudged him in the ribs.

"You look fabulous, as always." Holly winked at

her and waved at the table. "Go and sit down. Food will be ready any minute."

"*Carla!*" A sudden shrieking cry made Celia and Carter both jump. Holly laughed. "Sorry about that." She waved to the ceiling. A gray parrot was shuffling along one of the wooden beams. His clear gray eyes studied them seriously.

"That's Anthony. He's an African gray parrot. I inherited him. He belonged to Stefano's father. They can live to be over a hundred years old. Anthony is only thirty-seven." She clicked her tongue and pointed at a cage nestled in the corner of the patio, and the parrot flew from the beam to the cage. "He might even outlive me."

"Who's Carla?" Carter asked, watching the bird in fascination.

Holly laughed. "Stefano's father's mistress. From what Stefano told me, the parrot was there when Stefano's mother came screaming in the room, yelling *Carla* over and over again. Anthony can say a lot of words and phrases, but ever since then, shouting *Carla* seems to bring him the most joy."

Celia giggled, imagining how awkward it would have to be to live with a parrot screaming your mistress's name.

"Stefano's father gave us Anthony soon after that."

"I'll bet." Carter laughed and reached for a bottle of wine on the table. "Drinks?" He hovered near a trio of empty wineglasses.

"Yes, that would be lovely," Holly said. Carter poured the wine before passing around the salad bowl and starting the meal. Celia took a drink of her wine and watched Carter over the rim of her glass. He looked so calm, so relaxed. In England he always seemed on edge of late, but given his worries over his father's health and his job, she could understand. But right now she was giving him a moment to just be himself and he was giving her the gift of joy just by being here.

Celia spent most of the dinner watching Aunt Holly draw Carter out of his usual reserved behavior. By the end of the second course, Carter was telling Holly about the numerous times that he, Tristan, and Celia had gotten into trouble as children.

Carter's eyes glinted with mischief. "But my favorite story is when Tristan and I rigged several suits of armor in the great hall to move whenever Celia walked by. Every time she screamed, we just about keeled over with laughter."

"You two were terrible," Celia insisted, half laughing. "I spent weeks terrified that I would wake up and find one of those things clanking into my room."

"And then there were the fairy circles," Carter added.

Celia remembered that as well. She'd been only eight when she'd stumbled across a small carved circle of stones in the woods. A plate of teacakes had sat in the center, and she'd taken a few nibbles. When she'd returned home and told her nanny, the nanny had insisted that she was now the property of the Fae folk because she'd tasted their bread.

"Tristan had pinched a bottle of sherry from his father's study and gifted it to Celia's nurse so she would play along. The woman did a fine job."

"Too fine, if you ask me." Celia blushed, thinking about all the time she'd spent leaving gifts in the fairy circle in hopes of buying their mercy. Coins, biscuits, books. They'd all vanished from the circle each night. Then she'd caught Carter and Tristan tucking the items behind a tapestry that led down a hidden passageway. She'd been furious with them.

"You were so bloody adorable, believing in fairies." Carter poured her more wine, and Celia rolled her eyes.

"There is nothing wrong with believing in magic as a child," she insisted.

"There's nothing wrong with believing in magic as an adult," Holly added. She stood and waved a bottle of pale liquid that looked a bit like lemonade.

"Limoncello? Helps with digestion."

Celia and Carter accepted two shot glasses of limoncello. Carter threw his glass back and licked his lips. Celia did the same, then coughed violently as she choked on the drink. Limoncello was stronger than she'd expected.

"Easy, dear." Holly patted her back lightly as she snatched her water glass and gulped it down. She shot Carter a dirty look when he looked ready to laugh at her misfortune.

"Would you like some gelato for dessert?" Holly offered.

"Oh yes, I'd love some." Celia also hoped it might help wash down the aftertaste of the limoncello. Holly headed back inside the house. Carter got up and returned to the record player, sifting through the records. "Choose something good," she told him.

"As you wish." He flashed her a wicked grin and put on a new record. When the music started, she almost laughed in delight. It was one of her favorites, and she had a feeling he knew that. Carter held out a hand to her.

"Dance with me?"

Her heart skittered wildly as she placed her hand in his and he curled his fingers around her palm. He wound his arm around her waist and pulled her close. Lust and desire stole through her in a slow-burning wave as she followed his steps. She should have been disturbed by her attraction to him, but it no longer came as a surprise. She'd been aware of this man all her life. She knew him almost as well she knew herself, except she didn't know him like this—as a potential lover. Being in his arms, dancing to a soft classic song, she yearned to learn every one of his kisses. She tilted her face back, watching as his eyes lowered to her mouth.

"Celia...," he whispered with gentle reverence.

"I love the way you say my name." She wet her lips with her tongue. He was so at home in his body, with his sexuality, unlike her. She had learned to be a proper English lady. The niece to an earl. She was not supposed to be a wild, sexual being which meant she barely knew what she was doing. She'd had two boyfriends, one at university and one just after she graduated, and had enjoyed casual sex with both. But she'd only ever wanted, ever truly, wildly hungered for one man. And now she had him, at least for a while. So why was she still holding back?

"Do you know how long I've dreamed about this?" she asked.

"Not as long as I have," he replied.

"You sure about that?"

He lowered his head until their temples touched as he guided her around in a delicate circle. He softly hummed the words to the song. "Come a little bit closer...I'm all alone, and the night is so young..."

"The night is so young," she echoed, closing the distance between their mouths.

The kiss was soft, yet it exploded through her, making her insatiable with a craving for everything that kiss promised. He coaxed her lips apart, and their tongues met in a playful, sensual dance, just like their bodies. She could taste the sweet lingering limoncello on his lips, which she much preferred to drinking it herself.

He let go of her waist, and his fingers combed through her hair, clenching in the strands at the base of her neck. He gazed down at her as their mouths parted.

"You taste divine." He nuzzled her neck, mur-

muring soft, sweet words in her ear as he pressed his lips to her throat and cheek.

"Carter, I want you. I want you so much," she admitted. She blushed as he raised his head and flashed her that bad-boy grin, which melted away any notion of her being a well-behaved woman. It was the sort of smile that made her want to shout at the top of her lungs, listening to the sound of his laughter echo off the trees in the ancient woods outside the Pembroke estate.

Carter's eyes gleamed. He spun her out on one hand before pulling her back into his arms as they started to dance once again.

"We will go slow," he promised. "I want every memory to be perfect, and I'm not going to rush this, no matter how much you beg me."

From his cage, Anthony bobbed his head and whistled softly before chanting, "Beg me, beg me."

Celia and Carter burst out laughing. In that moment, Celia knew that being here with Carter for a month, taking it slow and making the most of their time together, was going to be worth it.

It was just as aunt had said. There was nothing wrong with believing in magic...even as an adult.

⚜

Holly lingered in the doorway, three cups of gelato sitting on a tray, as she watched her niece and Carter dancing and kissing. She returned to the kitchen and set their cups in the freezer, shaking her head and chuckling. The last thing she wanted to do was interrupt. Her niece needed this. The poor girl had always put everyone before herself, and coming here with Carter was not the Celia she knew. But it should be. Celia and that boy...they glowed.

Holly dipped a spoon into her gelato, watching the two young lovers discreetly from inside the house. Carter spun Celia around in a well-executed twirl and pulled her back into his arms. Holly sighed, her heart full of love and sorrow. Lord, she missed dancing. Stefano had been a perfect partner, and she'd never tried to lead or even stepped on his feet once. A man who knew how to dance could woo the world.

She looked at the framed photo of her and Stefano by the sink. They were standing beneath the arches of a church, white doves flying above them. The sky was split with strips of wispy stratus clouds. They'd had only a handful of years together, but she wouldn't trade them for anything.

Holly looked back at Celia, her heart tightening as she thought about what those two would face if they couldn't find a way to be together. A life without love wasn't a life at all.

❧ 6 ❦

Carter slipped out of his bedroom and paused at Celia's closed door. He could hear her on the phone talking to Matthew, telling him about Holly's home in the countryside and about Anthony the parrot. Her laughter made him grin. She was happy here, and that was what mattered right now.

Not wanting to eavesdrop, he decided to explore the house a bit more before turning in. The halls were decorated with expensive, old Renaissance paintings. It wouldn't surprise him to learn some of these originals were by Italian masters. He paused to examine a Roman marble bust tucked away in an alcove. He'd always thought the way the artists left the eyes blank was a little disconcerting. He'd read that most antique marble busts and statues had once been painted, but one couldn't detect those colors without using ultraviolet light, the paints having long since faded and flaked off.

"Not a fan?" Holly's voice behind him made him jump. She laughed and nodded at the bust. "Sorry. I saw you having a staring contest with him."

"Yes, I suppose I was." He laughed and followed Holly into the living room.

She retrieved a bottle of brandy from a cart in the corner. "Drink?"

"Thank you." He walked over to a wall of bookshelves next to the large flat-screen TV. He studied the old books, noticing a number of paperback romances tucked away haphazardly between hundred-year-old tomes.

"Here." Holly handed him a glass. He swirled the brandy before taking a sip. "Is Celia asleep?"

"Not yet. She's on the phone with Matthew."

Carter's gaze drifted to a framed photo of Holly and a handsome Italian man. They were staring into each other's eyes, lost to the world around them. He knew Holly's pain for losing Stefano, because he felt the same every time he looked at Celia. This picture might as well be of him and Celia, and in a month it would be all he had left of her.

"You miss him," Carter said.

"More than you can imagine." Holly sighed and took a drink. "So...you and my niece. Care to explain?"

He shouldn't have been surprised that Holly would ask him.

"I know she is...well... I know what this looks like. I know it all too well. It's just...well, it's complicated."

Holly lightly touched his shoulder. "That's an understatement. But I want to know *why* you two fled London, and why you only have a month. Celia was going to tell me, but I'd rather hear from you. For the record, I think you are just right for her."

Carter exhaled, still looking at the photo of Holly and Stefano.

"Eton asked Matthew to leave after he got into a fight with some boys bullying him. Seems he beat up a rather priggish son of an influential viscount who donates to the school. So he applied to Ravenswood which has a focus on math and science, his areas of specialty and they're fantastic at working with autistic students and getting them connected so they make connections which lead to careers. Celia said Matthew hasn't been this excited about schooling in a long time."

Holly swirled her glass, watching him intently. "I've heard of Ravenswood. But what does that have to do with Celia?"

"Well...it isn't my place to say, but suffice it to say that Celia has become responsible, financially, for Matthew's tuition. The academy isn't something they can afford using funds from the National Health Service. It's a school that operates entirely on a private basis with high tuition."

"What? Don't tell me that my brother... He did something foolish, didn't he?" Holly growled in frustration.

"Yes, very foolish, and Celia is paying for it."

"That explains much. I'd wondered why he moved onto Edward's estate." She smiled at Carter's reaction. "Oh, I'm not completely out of touch with affairs in England. I just don't usually bother myself with them. I won't inquire as to the details, however. So Celia is taking care of Matthew now? I suppose she always did, really. And she can't afford Ravenswood?"

He faced Holly. "She got a position at an architecture firm in London, but it isn't enough, and I..." He closed his eyes briefly. "I don't make even half what the firm is paying her. We can't afford Ravenswood's tuition, even if we combined all our resources together."

Holly's gaze softened. "But she found a way, didn't she?"

"Yes. She has agreed to marry Callum Radcliffe. He's a future earl and heir to a vast fortune."

"But she doesn't love him."

Heat flamed his face. "No. It's not a love match, for either of them. Callum has certain responsibilities, and he cannot marry the person he loves without destroying his relationship with his parents."

"Oh..." Holly covered her mouth. "Oh dear..."

"Yes," Carter agreed. "Callum's a good man, but he needs an heir."

"And Celia will do anything to help Matthew," Holly added. "And so, an arrangement was made. How positively medieval."

"She and Callum agreed to take a month to be with the people they love."

The word made her eyebrow arch. "Love?"

Carter knew his face was even redder now. "For a long time now. But neither of us felt we could approach the other. I'm just a steward's son, after all."

Holly huffed. "As if that matters. This isn't bloody *Downton Abbey*, you know." Before Carter could explain, she raised her hand. "No, I understand. No doubt my brother filled Celia's head with similar nonsense as your father did yours. Station and duty and all that rot. So, when this month is up...?"

"They will announce their engagement, and that's it. No more..." He waved a hand at the villa.

Holly's shoulders sagged. "I'd offer Celia the money, but I fear I don't have much. Stefano left me the villa, but I don't have much in the way of income." She glanced furtively around. "I've taken up a job of translating romance novels into Italian. It pays enough to handle my expenses here."

"Translating novels?" Carter asked. "That's brilliant."

She blushed. "Thank you. It is rather fun, I admit. But I wish I could help Celia...though I doubt she'd be willing to take any support from me."

"Probably not," he agreed. "She feels the need to be the one to acquire the money and not owe anyone. She sees her agreement with Callum as a fair trade."

"So the two of you finally admitted your feelings

and are going to spend what time you can together before she martyrs herself." Holly picked up the photo of her and Stefano, one that showed them posing beside an African bungalow where they'd gone on their honeymoon. She brushed her thumb over their faces, sighing. "We have so little time with the ones we love. How can she put a limit on that so willingly?"

"She feels she's the only one who can help Matthew. She might be right."

Holly set the photo back down and placed a hand on his shoulder. "I'm sorry."

"I'm sorry too," Carter said. "There's nothing I wouldn't do for her, give her, but money is the one thing I don't have. Tristan and I are trying to get the Pembroke estate noticed as a filming location by Hollywood producers, but it's a long process. It might never pay off."

"She doesn't need your money, Carter. I saw the way she looked at you tonight. She just wants you."

"If only it were that simple."

Holly shrugged. "Who knows? A lot can happen in a month."

"I suppose." The problem was, it would take a miracle to rescue her from this.

"I know you only have a month, but if you want my advice? Why don't you two watch a movie and relax tonight? I've got work to do, and there's no need for me to be in the way." Holly winked at him. "Oh, you can take one of my cars into Siena tomorrow. Show her the city. You know how much she loves history."

"Thank you, Holly." He meant it. Holly had given him and Celia a place of refuge to enjoy their time together.

After Holly left, he headed to his room to change, then knocked on Celia's door.

"Your aunt suggested we watch a movie. Interested?" he said through the closed door. It opened, and Celia smiled at him.

"Sure. I'll meet you there." She shut her door, and Carter headed back to the living room. He scanned the rows of movies on one of the bookshelves and smiled as he pulled one out. *Gone with the Wind*. He remembered Celia had had a framed poster of Rhett and Scarlett framed in her room for years when she'd been younger.

He turned on the TV and queued up the movie just as Celia joined him. She had changed out of her green dress and into a pair of shorts and a loose red short-sleeved blouse that she left untucked. Damn, the woman could make such a simple outfit seem like the most erotic thing he'd ever seen. She was bare-foot, and he had to work to control his sudden arousal at the sight of those long, curvy legs. Somehow she looked even sexier now than she had out by the pool in that teasing red bikini.

He cleared his throat, noting that she was just as carefully studying him. "Hey."

"Hey." She glanced at the TV. "*Gone with the Wind?* I love this movie!" She almost bounced as she hopped onto the couch, sinking back into the beige cushions and throwing her arms behind her head in a mock pose of relaxation. He couldn't help but laugh.

Her face turned pink with an adorable blush. "What?"

"I don't think I've ever seen you like this."

"Like what?"

"Relaxed." He had seen her tense and on edge most of her life. Only fleeting moments in their childhood came to mind where he'd seen Celia as she should be, relaxed and carefree. He remembered twelve-year-old Celia sitting on the branch of an old oak tree, her legs swinging as she talked about pirate ships in the history book she was reading for a school paper. He could have listened to her talk for hours.

"I have to try, don't I? Besides, if I can't relax here of all places, then I have problems." She patted the space on the couch next to her. "Sit, or you will block my view of Clark Gable, and I simply cannot allow that." She declared this with such sweet determination that he had to physically stop himself from going over to the couch and kissing her straight away.

"Yes, ma'am." He did his best courtly southern American accent as the movie began to play.

He took a seat next to Celia and pulled up the footrest so they could prop their feet up together. Celia reached for a light throw blanket and spread it over their legs. He leaned back into the cushions, holding his breath, wondering what Celia would do next. A few minutes into the movie, she shifted closer, though still not touching him. Another few minutes passed, and she moved another inch. He let her sidle closer two more times before he curled his arm around her shoulders and slid her against him.

"You were taking too long," he said when she looked at him in surprise.

"I'm sorry. I'm just so..." She didn't seem to know what to say. "I know what I said before about taking it slow, but could you...take control sometimes?"

He raised his brows. "By control you mean...?"

"I'm afraid if I go too slow I'll end up in reverse. If I don't go about this right, I want you to take control. I feel so nervous about this, but I want it so much. I trust your judgment."

He cupped her face, brushing the pad of his thumb over her lips.

"Thank you for being honest. And don't worry, I'll be happy to, as long as you promise to tell me if I go too fast." He offered her his hand. "Deal?"

"Deal." She shook his hand, and then she wrapped an arm around his waist and put her head on his chest.

Carter was filled with an intense sense of warmth.

He couldn't remember a time he hadn't been so in love with her. And now here he was. With her. He laid his head back on the couch and sighed in contentment.

They reached the intermission, and the sweeping musical score surrounded them. "Why do you love this movie?" he asked her.

Celia rubbed her cheek against his chest. "Because Scarlett meets the man of her dreams, a scoundrel, a man who takes what he wants with no regrets and yet loves deeply and passionately."

"But she loses him in the end. She drives him away." Carter went quiet as he realized the eerie parallel of Rhett and Scarlett to him and Celia.

"She does," Celia admitted. "Foolishly so. But, you know, *tomorrow is another day*."

For an instant he pictured Celia in the late 1800s, wearing a torn gown, leaning against an open doorway, searching not for Rhett but for him, vowing she would find a way to win him back.

When the movie continued, Celia rubbed her hand on his stomach in slow strokes, in an almost absentminded way. But her touch set him on fire, and he had to think of every dull thing in his life to try to control his body's reactions.

Was it time to speed things up? He caught her hand on his stomach and lifted it to his lips. He kissed the back of her knuckles and then turned her hand over so he could press a light kiss to her wrist. She smelled like vanilla and honeysuckle, and he wanted to ask her how women did that, especially her. It was as though she knew his weakness. Honeysuckle was like a drug to him. When he and Celia were fourteen, they had stolen a moment together in the gardens beneath a trellis covered in wisteria, surrounded by honeysuckle.

So many times he had closed his eyes over the years, smelling that scent and remembering the feel of her soft lips against his. It had been hotter than any fantasy he'd ever had, to remember that moment and wonder what other kisses with her over the years could've been like. Now he had the chance to make up for a lifetime of missed kisses.

Carter cupped her face again as he lowered his head toward hers. His mind, his body, even his soul belonged to this woman, and he wanted her to feel that on his lips. Years of longing for each other had simmered between them. He nestled her in a protective embrace as their lips finally met. Heat settled in his groin, reminding him how much he craved her. She sighed against him and wrapped her arms around his neck.

She wasn't as experienced as he was, but she exhibited a raw sensuality that bewitched him like no woman ever had. He let his hands explore the slopes of her breasts, the valley of her hips, and the gossamer feel of her honey-blonde hair between his fingers. He wanted to spend forever kissing her long, elegant throat until he found the spot that made her body ignite with unquenchable desire.

Her legs were smooth satin under his hands, and he groaned in delight as she moved to straddle him, her knees sliding onto either side of his hips. Her body molded to his, fire racing between them as the sensation of being so close threatened to overwhelm them both. His cock hardened, and she pulled herself into him, kissing him like she wanted to brand herself into his skin. Her breath whispered over his lips, and he cupped her bottom, squeezing hard as she whimpered with desperate need. Their kiss was hard, then soft, then hard again as they explored each other's mouths, committing each and every moment to memory.

"I want you so much," she moaned against his mouth.

He gripped her bottom, urging her to grind her

self against him, knowing it would be sweet torture for him, but he wanted to see her come, see if he could affect her strongly enough that she climaxed from kisses and stimulation alone. It would take the edge off her hunger and still keep things slow enough that he wouldn't feel guilty for rushing things. At least, that was what he hoped, but when she bit his bottom lip and dragged her nails along his scalp at the back of his head, he couldn't stop himself. He urged her to move faster, to rub herself against him, because he wasn't going to last.

Celia gasped, stiffening against him, and he dug his hands into her bottom as his body went rigid and he came in his jeans like a randy teenager.

"Oh my...God," Celia panted. She clutched him as she buried her face in his neck, as though embarrassed.

"Fuck," he cursed. "You okay, love?" He cupped the back of her neck, breathing hard, his body flushing with heat and shame. He should have kept control, but there was no way he could have given what he felt with Celia.

She cupped his face. "Carter, I'm fine. But are you?"

"Yes, I'm fine," he promised as he gently removed her from his lap. "I just need to shower." He looked at the TV, which was now in the final stages of the ending of the movie.

"Shower?" Celia looked hurt. He leaned over to steal a swift kiss.

"You were so hot that I lost control. I need to tend to that. You know..." He couldn't say more.

"Oh?" She covered her mouth, eyes widening. "*Oh! Really?*" She started to giggle, but she stopped when she noticed his frown.

"It happens to the best of us, you know." He knew his tone was a bit too curt, but he didn't like being embarrassed. Was this how they were going to start their month together? He turned and left the living room. He was going to take a cold-as-fuck shower and try to remind his body who was in charge.

⚜

CELIA KNEW SHE'D ACTED SHAMELESSLY, RIDING Carter like a stallion, and now she had paid the price. They'd both gotten off while still fully clothed. How was that even possible? That was something her teenage self would have done, if she'd ever had the chance. And she'd embarrassed Carter in the process. Men had fragile egos, especially when it came to sex. She threw her head back on the couch and sighed. This was not how she wanted this month to go, but what had she expected? Thirty perfect days? That wasn't possible.

She watched the last few minutes of *Gone with the Wind*, hoping Carter might return, but he didn't. She turned off the TV and headed back to her room. She paused in her doorway and looked over her shoulder at Carter's closed door. Her heart twinged with regret. She'd been so happy, lost in those kisses, and when she'd climaxed, it had filled her with an almost otherworldly joy. She'd been relieved to know she wasn't the only one affected.

She changed into her silk short-sleeved pajamas and removed the pins from her hair, then sat down on her bed and pulled her laptop toward her. She had talked to Matthew earlier, and he had been excited to tell her about receiving his enrollment package for Ravenswood Academy. It was a boarding school, and she was glad Matthew was excited about the move. Being stuck in a small cottage with their parents would have been impossible in the long run. She would have a month when she got home to see him before he left. Celia picked up her phone and texted Callum.

Matthew received his enrollment package today. He's excited to go. Thank you.

She put the phone down and opened her laptop. She scanned her inbox and saw an email with a project in the subject line. She clicked it open and saw it was from one of the firm's top partners, Christopher Ridings.

She read through the email slowly, making mental notes. The firm was being hired by a Scottish lord named Garrick Kincade, who had a fifteenth-century castle that desperately needed a remodel. Parts of it even had to be rebuilt.

Rather than simply hire a construction crew, he wanted an architectural firm that could return his home to its former medieval glory. Lord Kincade was a member of the Scottish Parliament, and as such, he was very influential. If they could please him, it would be excellent for business.

Her boss, Mr. Ridings, was interested in having his new hires, like Celia, take a stab at the remodel. Celia replied back immediately that she would like to participate, and she asked for photos of the castle's exterior and interior, both of the current living resi-dence and the crumbling parts that needed remodel-ing. Ridings was giving everyone two weeks to craft a proposal for the exterior design as well as an interior remodeling concept.

Celia smiled as she closed her laptop. She knew she was supposed to be relaxing, spending her time with Carter, but this could be a huge opportunity. A chance to prove that she wasn't just an aristocrat with the right connections. She could show her firm she had real talent.

Her cell phone buzzed, and she checked it. Callum had texted back.

Callum: *Excellent. How are you doing?*

She hesitated before replying.

Celia: *I'm good. I'm glad we both took a month to sort things out.*

Callum: *Me too. Bryson is upset, but he's glad we have at least a little time.*

Celia's throat tightened as she replied.

Celia: *I know how he feels. But what else can we do?*

Callum: *I don't know.*

She waited a moment again before texting him one last time.

Celia: *Enjoy every minute.*

Callum: *I will. You too.*

Celia's gaze drifted toward the fresco opposite her bed. She hadn't noticed it before. A pair of lovers were in a passionate embrace, their colorful robes gleamed in the lamplight. The small tiles were freshly painted, but the style was old, as though the artist wanted to channel two-thousand-year-old frescoes from the Roman Empire. Strangely, it made her think of Carter.

She closed her laptop and climbed off her bed. She didn't want to sleep alone, not one night. If he was upset about what had happened, she would convince him not to be.

She turned off the lights in her room and walked across the hall to his. She was about to knock, but then she thought better of it. He could turn her way easier if she knocked. Celia opened the door. Carter was sitting up in bed, a book in his hands. She stared at him, surprised to see a pair of rimless glasses on his face. She hadn't known he wore glasses. But of course, she'd never seen him at night in bed.

They stared at each other for a long second before he crooked his finger at her, beckoning her to come. She stepped into the room and closed the door behind her. She tiptoed over—for whose benefit she had no idea—and he pulled back the covers on the side closest to her.

She slid in beside him. "I didn't know you wore glasses."

Carter chuckled, touching the rims self-consciously. "Just for reading. The doctor prescribed me contacts for daytime. It's probably because I squint so much at my computer when I'm working. Eyestrain or some such."

She leaned against his arm, smiling at him. "I like them. Very sexy."

He chuckled sarcastically. "I'll bet."

"I'm serious!" she insisted. "I really do like them." She pressed her cheek against his shoulder. He wore a gray T-shirt and pajama pants. Perfectly ordinary, and yet right now it was the sexiest outfit ever. She pulled the book from his hands and looked at the cover.

"*Lady Viola and the Dashing Duke?* Romance?" Carter was reading a steamy romance novel? It seemed so unlike him. But then, perhaps that was where he'd picked up his moves that made her melt into a puddle whenever she was in his arms.

"It's an English copy of one of the books your aunt translated into Italian. According to the foreword, it's a reprint of a book written in the early 1800s. Gothic romance. A bit edgy for its day, I imagine. I thought it might hold my interest. I left my paperbacks at home, and my e-reader is still charging." He nodded at the nightstand, where his reader was plugged into the wall.

"Would you read to me?"

Carter looked at her in surprise.

"If you wish."

She nodded eagerly, settling more comfortably against him.

He started to read. Celia closed her eyes, letting his deep, seductive voice sweep her away.

Before she knew it, she was falling asleep, truly relaxed, truly content for perhaps the first time in her entire life.

❧ 7 ❧

Celia woke slowly, sunlight coloring the backs of her eyelids gold. She was warm, safe, and happy. A dozen other softer, sweeter emotions ran beneath her skin like rivers of heat and light. She nuzzled deeper into her pillow, and her pillow grunted.

She opened one eye. Her pillow was actually Carter's chest. She froze. She was in bed beside him, her body twined with his, clutching his chest like a favorite stuffed animal. After the initial shock, that thought made her smile.

Carter threaded his fingers through the strands of her hair in a gentle, undemanding way. It felt like they'd done this a thousand times, that she'd woken up against his bare skin, feeling the heat of him like this, and he'd always been touching her with such gentle possession. It was as though they were made to lie together, two halves of a perfect whole.

Celia's throat tightened, and she struggled to contain her desire and afraid this moment would end.

"Been awake long?" she asked. She raised her head to rest her chin on his chest.

"Only a few minutes." He smiled at her, and she was warm all over again, but this time the sun had nothing to do with it. "I was enjoying watching you sleep."

She started to smile, but soon panic took over. Had she been snoring? Her hair had to be all over the place right now. She should probably dash for the bathroom and brush her teeth...

"Celia, stop worrying. You're bloody gorgeous."

"How did you—?"

"I can see it in your eyes. *Oh my God, I must look like a mess.*" His fingers in her hair tightened slightly as his gaze held hers for a long, intense moment.

"You always could read my mind," she said. She wished more than anything that she could read his the same way.

"I've spent my whole life watching you," he admitted. "Wanting you..." The words hung in the air between them, but she was too afraid to echo them back, at least right now.

After a long moment, she cleared her throat. "What time is it?" She looked around for a clock. Carter reached over to the nightstand to check his wristwatch and squinted.

"Eight thirty." He sighed, dropping the watch and turning back to her, his arms magically cradling her body against his. How did men know how to do that, move a woman's body into the right spot like that? She felt his arousal pressed against her thigh, which made her blush, but he didn't seem embarrassed. She wondered if he might kiss her as their noses brushed, but instead he groaned softly.

"We should get up."

"We should," she agreed. She put no urgency in her words, praying for him to move a little closer.

"We really should." He rested his forehead against hers, and she practically melted against him. "Holly mentioned last night that we could take her car and drive into Siena. What do you think?"

She breathed in, taking in his addictive scent one more time before she pushed herself away from him. One of them had to get out of this bed first.

"Sounds good to me. I'll go showe—" She tried to get up, but Carter rolled her beneath him, his mouth capturing her startled squeak of delight. He pinned her wrists to the bed on either side of her head and coaxed her body into a fiery desire with a claiming, yet playful kiss. His hips settled between her thighs, and he rocked against her, pressing his erection against her pajama shorts. She locked her legs around his waist, needing to feel him even closer. They kissed, grinding against each other before she felt that familiar surge of pleasure just within reach. Carter bit her lip, then thrust his tongue inside while pressing down on her hips in a way that made her explode with a muffled cry. Carter gasped her name seconds later and smiled, almost shyly. They caught their breath, settling against each other in comfort, yet she wanted more of him than ever before. And bloody hell, they were still stuck in his bed. Not that she wanted to be anywhere else.

"At some point, we're actually going to do this without clothes, right? Naked and all?" she asked between panting breaths.

"Naked and all?" he echoed with a chuckle.

"Yeah, like you and me, naked. You know…"

Carter laughed and placed his forehead against hers. "Oh, we definitely will. I'm just giving you a taste, love." He let go of her wrists, stole one more kiss, and rolled out of bed. He shot her a wicked grin as he disappeared into his bathroom. Celia grabbed his pillow and covered her face to muffle a groan. *Naked and all? Geeze.* She climbed out of the bed and returned to her own room.

By the time she showered and dressed, Carter was waiting for her in the kitchen. They had a quick breakfast of eggs and toast before they left. Carter picked up a set of keys from a colorful blown glass bowl on a side table by the door.

He tossed her the keys, and she saw the Aston Martin logo on the key fob. "Apparently, your aunt has a classic Aston she's kept in perfect condition. She has fine taste in cars."

And I have good taste in men, Celia thought as she returned the keys to Carter. He wore jeans and a navy-blue T-shirt, which clung to his lean body like a second skin. The man was all slick muscle and leonine grace. She was spellbound by the way the sunlight caught his hair, making the tousled strands gleam. She wanted to fist her hands in his hair and drag his head down to hers, but she needed to behave today. She didn't trust herself not to mess things up royally where Carter was concerned.

She followed him to the front of the villa and saw the metallic gray two-seater sports car, top down, ready to go. Carter reached into the car and pulled out a multicolored scarf.

"Holly recommended you use this for your hair if we leave the top down." He handed it to her, slightly baffled.

She took the silk scarf with a laugh. She folded it into a triangle and covered her head. It would keep her hair from getting windblown during the drive. Celia bit back a grin as Carter, in a display of chivalry, rushed to open the door for her. His eyes trailed along her legs a second longer than was decent as she slid into the seat. He'd always done that, let his looks linger longer than was proper, and she knew she'd often done the same. But now they didn't have to hide that desire from each other or anyone else.

He slid into the driver's seat and started the engine, which purred like a contented cat until Carter hit the gas pedal and it roared to life. They shot out of the curved drive and headed for the road that would take them to Siena.

Celia held a hand out of the car, laughing as the wind rushed through her fingers and the sun warmed her skin. The rolling hills around them were a mixture of brilliant greens and stunning golds. Every so often they saw another villa on a hill or tucked in a valley as they zipped through the narrow streets of small towns that were half a millennium old.

Carter reached for her other hand, and they laced their fingers together. He glanced her way, smiling broadly, and she couldn't help but smile back.

It was close to noon when they reached the outskirts of Siena, where Carter found a lot to park the car. They would have to walk the rest of the way because most of Siena, especially the city center, was pedestrian only.

Celia was amazed by the rustic Renaissance architecture and the stunning courtyards adorned with flowers climbing up old wooden trellises. There they walked through narrow alleys behind buildings which ascended up to gorgeous rooftop views. Thecloudless sky was a pure blue like the ceiling of a painted church dome. Red and yellow flags hung suspended over the winding streets, their thin silk illuminated from behind by the sun. The city itself was at the top of the hill, stretching out in three different directions from the main square called Piazza del Campo.

"God, this is beautiful," said Carter. They were still holding hands, and she felt like a lovesick teen for adoring that simple connection. "I mean, I've seen pictures, but..."

"You've never been to Italy?" she asked.

Carter shook his head. "I've always had an up-to-date passport but I've never left England before."

"What? But surely Tristan would have..." Her cousin had traveled quite a bit. Before he'd met Kat, he'd traveled the world over looking for thrills or women to woo and bed. Given how close they were, it surprised Celia to learn that Carter hadn't gone with him on any of these trips.

"Oh, he offered, but I never went. My rule was that I wouldn't go on any trip unless I could afford it."

Carter had flown coach to Italy, but she had assumed that was to avoid attracting unwanted attention from her parents. After all, they would have recorded him as a passenger on her uncle's private jet, and that might lead to questions. But it seemed it had been as much about pride as propriety. He spoke again more softly.

"One day I will find a way to pay you and Holly back for letting me stay with you like this." He looked so...ashamed. In all the years she'd known Carter, he'd never looked embarrassed by his financial circumstances before, and she hated herself for making him feel that way. She hadn't wanted to remind him of the disparity between their social circles. Given that her own family was all but penniless now, it shouldn't matter to him, but it did.

She pulled him to a stop. "You don't need to pay anyone back. Consider it a gift."

His lips curved in an almost biting smile. "I guess I'm Julia Roberts in this *Pretty Woman* scenario, aren't I?"

Celia frowned. "You aren't a prostitute, Carter."

He chuckled a bit coldly, looking away. "Then what do you call bringing me here to fulfill your sexual fantasies?"

Celia dropped his hand, pain shooting to her heart so strongly that she winced.

"You know that it isn't like that." She paused. "If you really believe that, you are a bloody idiot, and I want you to take me straight back to Holly's." She craved him on so many levels, not just physically, but if he was going to ruin this by lashing out like a hurt child, she wouldn't stand for it. She'd thought these were his fantasies too, that she wasn't in this desire and longing alone. Carter reached out, gripping both of her hands before she could pull away.

"I'm sorry. I didn't mean it. I just want to contribute. It's important to me. I don't want to owe anyone, especially not you."

"We both owe my aunt. That's the only thing you can feel guilty about."

He nodded, pulling her close to him, and bent his head.

"Being with you here isn't about a fantasy," she said softly. "It's about experiencing a dream before I have to let go. You know how I feel..." She wanted to make him understand that she didn't want to use him. Being with him was a dream come true. If only there was some way to turn it into a reality.

"I know," he replied. "I know." His focus dropped to her lips. She met him halfway and melted into a heated kiss between them.

The sound of catcalling broke them apart. Two young Italian men were standing outside a café watching them. The young men laughed and clapped as they chattered in Italian. Celia knew enough Italian to blush at the content of their comments.

"We should go." She grasped Carter's hand, and they quickly crossed the street, ignoring the men's jeers. It was mortifying, but she knew it was fairly normal here. Men were vocal about women and their interest in them. It was not her favorite part of Italian culture. Carter shot the group of men a chilling look as he and Celia left.

They reached the square, Piazza del Campo, and Carter's eyes widened at the massive space, full of locals and tourists mingling. Dozens of people were stretched out on the red-bricked plaza as though they were sunning on a tropical beach. Celia gazed out upon the square and city hall, its looming tower dominating the square. The whole square angled slightly downward in a gradual, slow architectural flow designed to draw the tourist's eye to the city hall, or Palazzo Pubblico. Celia had read a tour book on the flight over, loving the rich medieval history of Siena.

She'd read that the square had been the focus of the town's society in medieval times. The tower in city hall bore a stylized sun, and it had been built around 1340. Flanking the sun logo were she-wolf gargoyles that seem to crawl out of the stone and snarl at the people below. They were supposed to represent the she-wolf who had suckled Romulus and Remus, the founders of Rome according to legend. It was said that Remus's son was the man who in turn founded the city of Siena.

Carter watched her get lost in the history of the city for a moment. "What do you want to do next?"

"Why don't we have a quiet lunch at a café and then go to the Piazza del Duomo?" she suggested.

Carter pointed out a small café near the Piazza del Campo, where they ordered a pizza and two glasses of chianti. Carter raised his glass. "To Siena."

"To Siena." They clinked their glasses together. Celia watched the tourists and locals pass by the sunlit window, feeling strangely at home here. It was hard not to when the sun was so warm, and the smell of freshly cooked pasta and spices filled the air beneath the Gothic spires of the church that towered over the winding streets. When she looked to Carter, she saw him looking out the window as well, a wistful expression on his face.

"If you never had to go back to England, do you think you'd miss it?" she asked, knowing that a person who'd never left their country before could miss home deeply.

He smiled a little. "I honestly don't know." He sipped his wine before continuing. "I'd miss the heavy wet fog rolling through the gardens on some mornings and the way the rain sounds against the gables on the manor house in the early morning hours, tempting me to sleep in. But I wouldn't miss the worries and the pressure of my life there."

"Me too." Celia had forgotten just how hard he worked as the junior steward. She knew he had numerous responsibilities, but she wondered if he was taking on even more of his father's work to help him. If he was, it would explain much of the tension and worry she'd seen him carrying these last few months.

They drank their wine in companionable silence. With anyone else she would've felt compelled to make small talk, but this was Carter. She'd known him all her life. There was no awkwardness with him, not like with other men.

After lunch they ventured down a side alley, where they found a small art gallery. Celia studied both the modern art and the more old-fashioned portraits. She stopped when she saw a portrait of a woman in a pale-blue Victorian gown seated at a desk, pencil in hand as she wrote. Sunlight from the windows bathed her desk in gold, while the background behind her was in dark shadows. The title of the work was *The Dreamer*. She was captivated.

"She's lovely. She looks real enough that I could reach out and touch her," Carter murmured from behind her.

"Yes...it's magical." She saw the price tag on the painting and was tempted to buy it. It would be an expense, but having *The Dreamer* in her office somehow seemed important, like a quiet but powerful muse. But she couldn't afford it.

"Let's go see the cathedral." She took Carter's hand, and they walked to the Piazza del Duomo. The thirteenth-century Gothic cathedral had a striped bell tower and was covered with statues. Every inch of bare surface was layered with frescoes and art. The church was a kaleidoscope of green, white, pink, and gold. She took mental notes of the blend of architectural styles, the lower portions of the church featuring remnants of the fading Romanesque style with its round arches and the pointed arches of the newer Gothic style with frilly designs lacing the pointed peaks.

"Wow." Carter looked impressed.

Celia grinned. "You see the six-story bell tower?" She pointed to the tower at the back of the church. "It looks taller than it is because of an optical illusion. The white marble stripes get narrower toward the top, which makes it seem farther away."

Carter pointed to the she-wolves above the main entrance of the cathedral. "Are those wolves?"

"Yes, they are there to honor Romulus and Remus."

"Oh, right, the founders of Rome." He eyed the she-wolves with open appreciation.

She and Carter spent over two hours touring the church, the baptistery, the crypt, and the church museum before they explored more of the historical squares in the city. By the time they were ready for dinner, her mind was abuzz with fresh architectural ideas.

"Do you want to stay in town for dinner?" she asked.

"I do if you do."

"Holly recommended one of her favorite restaurants called Vernice and Giuseppe. She said it serves modern Tuscan cuisine in a chic Gothic grotto."

"A grotto?" Carter looked at her quizzically. She grinned, delighted that she'd caught his attention. She wanted to take him to all the special places she could while he was here, and this one would certainly be unique given its ancient history.

"It's a medieval vault. They supposedly have a wine cellar that dates back to Etruscan times, long before the Romans were here."

His brows rose, and he smiled back. "Lead the way."

Celia took them back to the Piazza del Campo near city hall, where they found signs leading them down into the underground restaurant. The air was cool, and the craggy stone walls were very much like a grotto. A waiter showed them to a booth that had candles and fresh flowers in a short round vase, giving the table a romantic feel. Celia grew nervous. Lunches in cafés were one thing, but romantic candlelit dinners? This felt too serious. What kind of message was she sending?

Carter slid into the booth opposite her. "You okay?"

She blushed and reached for the wine menu. "It's nothing, just the dim light." She found what she wanted and passed the list to Carter. "I'll have a glass of the Côte du Rhône."

"Same for me." Carter handed the wine list back to the waiter as Celia studied the menu. Between waking up in their quiet, comfortable intimacy to the tour of the city, they'd had such an amazing day. It was just the way she'd hoped their time here would be, but she was still so nervous. This felt like a real date, which was silly given that she'd slept in his bed last night. Typically it went the other way around.

A finger slowly pulled the shield of her menu

down, and she met Carter's gaze. He watched her with an intensity that made her squirm in her seat, the kind of stare that could make a woman forget her name. If she gave a single word of encouragement, she imagined he'd take her to the nearest bathroom, and they'd...

She focused on his face again, banishing, at least for now, images of them having sex in the bathroom of a restaurant built in an ancient Italian grotto.

God, he looked so handsome. How could a man be this...gorgeous? Why had she denied herself this for so long? Had duty and family responsibilities really kept her from him? She felt as though her problems in England were melting away.

"What's wrong?"

"It's just..." She paused. "This is like a date."

He blinked, as though startled by her statement, but then he leaned forward to cup her chin. "This is most definitely a date."

"We've never been on a date."

His wickedly sweet smile made her knees weak. "No. We haven't. But we're going to make sure we enjoy it. Right?" He was the only man who ever made her forget where she was. When he looked at her like that, she couldn't help but picture him sweeping everything off the table and feasting on her instead. She wanted that so much she didn't realize the waiter had been standing beside her for at least a minute.

"*Ahem.*"

She flinched as she looked up to the patient waiter. "Sorry."

"What would you like?"

They ordered an antipasto of bruschetta and a primo piatto of carbonara, followed by a secondo piatto of steak to share.

Carter reached for a piece of bruschetta once it arrived. "So, tell me about your new job. We haven't had a chance to look at any of your designs yet."

The casual way he asked the question put her at ease, and she found herself excited to talk about her new project. "Oh! I'm actually working on a proposal while we're here."

Carter's forehead suddenly crinkled. "You're what? You're working? Now? On vacation?"

Celia smiled. "I've never been someone who leaves her job completely at home. I'm sure you can relate."

"I suppose I can," Carter said. "So, what are you working on?"

She couldn't rein in her enthusiasm. "A Scottish lord wants to have his fifteenth-century castle restored back to a fully functioning residence. Mr. Ridings is giving his junior architects a chance to submit a proposal. I really think I could win this—I have so many ideas."

"That sounds fantastic. What would you do for the restoration?" Carter offered her the plate of bruschetta, and she took a few bites before replying.

"Restoration isn't just about building a place back the way it was. You also need to modernize it in some ways." She spoke confidently now. This was a world she was comfortable with, one she felt she understood. "The challenge is to rebuild an old castle in a way that would feel new with updated functionality."

Carter leaned in. "Such as?"

"Well, let's say you re-panel the interior state rooms, and you match the mahogany base and silk wallpaper, but you can also add a speaker system and update the doors to have keyless entry locks, proper insulation against drafts, that sort of thing. But the key is..."

"To maintain the integrity of the original structure and its natural design," Carter guessed.

"Exactly."

"I guess the last thing you'd want is to overdo it

and make it look like some shoddy luxury hotel that confuses glitz with elegance."

She grinned. Carter had always understood her. "And you and Tristan—you're still trying to get movie producers interested in the estate, right?"

He nodded and leaned back as the waiter delivered their carbonara and steak. "Yes. I actually have some work to do on that as well."

Celia feigned shock. "What? *You're* working on vacation?"

Carter chuckled. "I just wanted to adjust some of the language in the package we've been sending out. The pitch needs more of a punch to be effective."

"Sounds like we both should plan to work a little tonight when we get back." There were other kinds of "work" she'd like to indulge in, but perhaps focusing on work for a few hours would make her miss him and hunger for him all the more. It would make being with him tonight that much sweeter.

They enjoyed a long, companionable silence as they finished their dinner. Despite the occasional attack of nerves, she felt entirely at ease around Carter, but maybe that came from having known him all her life. He'd had the chance to spend time around her because Tristan's father, seemed to have a soft spot for him and had let him grow up alongside Tristan with little concern about station or birth, at least until they were teenagers.

"Celia...," Carter began. "Did you know that your uncle knew my mother? I mean, not just knew her in the way a man knows the names of his staff, but...more so."

There was a troubled look on Carter's face, and she wondered why. Having her uncle on his side was a good thing. Lord Pembroke could be a powerful ally.

Celia tilted her head. That was news to her. "How do you mean?"

"I'm not sure. Before we left, I asked his permission for vacation time, and he mentioned how like my mother I am...even down to the color of my eyes.”

Celia stilled in sipping her wine. A man only remembered a woman's eyes if he had been in love with her. At least, that seemed to be why most men did.

“Do you think he was in love with her?” she asked quietly.

“In love? No...that...no. Given the way he felt about Tristan dating Kat, I can't picture him being in love with the wife of a steward.”

“But she wasn't *just* the wife of his steward. Your mother grew up on the estate and was close in age to my uncle. They might have known each other for years before your father came to work there.”

Now that she thought about it, she could picture her uncle, a young man driven by duty who could never marry the daughter of a butler. Something like that would have caused a devastating scandal to the family, especially back then. In a split second, she came to a realization.

Her uncle and Carter's mother may have faced a situation almost identical to their own. Two people who grew up together, who perhaps fell in love, but circumstances kept them worlds apart. And every time her uncle looked at Carter, he saw the woman he'd loved and lost. It made sense, but she was afraid to share this with Carter. She didn't want to upset him with the idea that his mother had loved someone other than his father.

Carter toyed with the stem of his wineglass, his gaze downcast. “I wish...” He drew in a heavy breath. “I wish she was still alive. Sometimes I worry that I'll forget her, you know?” There was such pain in his voice that she had to comfort him.

Celia reached across the table, curling her fingers around his wrist and squeezing gently. Carter had been only ten when his mother had succumbed to cancer.

"I wish I'd had a chance to know her better." Celia's heart fluttered as Carter turned his hand over and held his palm up to hold her hand, squeezing it back.

"She liked you—I remember that," Carter assured her with a wry smile.

After they finished their meal and paid the bill, they climbed the stairs hewn into the rock and exited into the cool night air.

"I smell rain," Celia said.

"So do I. We had better head back to the car." Carter took her hand, and they strolled down the meandering streets. Carter pointed out the visible constellations in the blanket of bright stars that peeped through the heavy storm clouds rolling in.

When they passed through the Piazza del Campo, Celia noticed the tourist crowds were thinning out, and the younger men and women were out dancing in the square to music.

"Well, we don't have to head straight to the car," Carter said with a smile, gesturing toward the festivities. "Shall we?"

Carter pulled Celia into the square to join the other couples, holding her close as they danced. The music was slow and sweet, yet seductive in the way that only Italian music could be. Celia tucked herself against his body, feeling his heartbeat against her cheek. The other couples moved around them, the sounds of their conversations blending with the music. Carter and Celia didn't speak; they simply danced, their breaths coming a little hotter, a little faster than normal as they pressed tighter together.

There was nothing more perfect than this. How could there be? The sounds of the string quartet echoing against the ancient stone of the medieval Italian square, the perfect movement between them, even the hint of coming rain upon the breeze. Celia wished she could trap this moment in a jar and keep it forever.

As the first few drops began to fall, the music ended and she and Carter broke apart, lingering for a moment longer while the magic of the night seemed to suspend itself in the air between them. She shivered a little. The longing she felt for *more* was so deep, so earnest that it rippled beneath her skin. *Soon,* she promised herself.

They began to walk back to the car and had another few streets to go when the rain clouds unleashed a torrent. They broke into a run, but Celia slipped on the cobblestones, crying out as her ankle twisted. She stopped and bent over, biting back a cry of pain as she tried to put pressure on it.

Carter knelt down in front of her and lifted her ankle up. "Let me see." She braced her hands on his shoulders while he looked her over.

The pain wasn't as intense as before. At least it wasn't broken. Carter's fingers explored her skin, and she wiped her face of rain as she tried to put weight on her foot again. She could, but she would have to walk far more slowly.

"I think I can walk, but—" She gasped as Carter scooped her up into his arms and carried her down the street. She wrapped her arms around his neck, delighted at being carried but also frustrated that she had tripped and was now playing the part of a distressed damsel—the last thing she'd ever wanted to be.

"Sorry."

Carter chuckled. "For giving me a chance to hold you like this? I'm not." He grinned at her.

By the time they reached the car, they were soaked to the bone. Carter opened her door and helped her inside. Then he got in and turned on the seat warmers. She was already starting to shiver.

"I wish I had a coat to give you," he said. It had

been so warm today that neither of them had come prepared.

"I'm fine," she promised. Once they got home, she planned to warm up in his arms for as long as possible. They left the hilltop city far behind them, like a glowing jewel nestled atop the dark Italian landscape.

Celia decided that tonight was the night. They had only twenty-nine days left, and she didn't want to waste any more time.

❦ 9 ❦

Carter held his breath as he and Celia slipped quietly into the dark villa. Celia's aunt was probably asleep. It was after ten, and they didn't want to wake her. Anthony stirred in his cage, his gray feathers rustling as he whistled softly.

"Hello there... Hello there." The eerie human-sounding words echoed in the living room.

"*Shhhh*," Celia whispered.

"Hush, Anthony, hush now," the bird whispered back and raised one foot up to his beak like he was telling them to be quiet instead. He shuffled along one of the bars, making soft clicking sounds as they passed by him. She and Carter paused in front of their separate bedroom doors, before Carter turned around and held out his other hand to her.

His heart raced. If she took his hand, he would make love to her tonight. Was it too soon? Was it time? How could he think that? Time was the one thing they no longer had in abundance. Celia gazed at his open palm for a long moment, then placed her hand in his. Without a word, he tugged her into his room and closed the door. No turning back now.

She stood there, her blonde hair in loose wet bands of gold down her shoulders, shaking as her wet clothes gave her a fresh chill.

"Why don't you take a hot shower?" Where he found the strength to suggest that instead of simply pulling her into his bed he would never know.

She nodded and placed a foot on his bed to remove her strappy gold sandals. Everything about her bewitched him, from those delicate pretty feet to the small scar above her collarbone she'd gotten from a fall out of a tree when she was twelve. They had been racing Tristan to the top of the tree. She was a few inches shorter, and when she'd lunged for a branch, she'd missed and plummeted to the ground.

Despite the sheen of tears he'd glimpsed in her eyes when he'd come to her rescue, she hadn't cry. She'd sniffed, picked herself up off the moss-covered ground, brushed her hands down her sweater, and smoothed out her pleated skirt. Even the cut on her collarbone was brushed off with quiet strength. It might have been then that he'd fallen in love with her —not that he could ever pinpoint the exact moment. It felt like he'd always loved her, as though it had been years in the making.

Celia set her sandals against the wall out of the way, and then removed her light-blue sweater. Beneath it she wore a floral-print dress that flared out at the hips into a full skirt, stopping just above her knees. She turned away from him and pulled her hair to one side of her neck, baring her back.

"Can you unzip my dress?" she asked him so sweetly, so innocently that it was going to kill him.

His hands almost shook as he reached for the zipper. The sound of the metal teeth unfastening was the only noise he could hear, aside from the patter of rain against the window. His hand stopped at her lower back, just above her bottom. She let the wet dress drop to the floor. Underneath, she wore only a pair of white lace panties and a matching lace bra.

Fuck, she was beautiful. So sexy, and she wasn't even trying.

She walked into the bathroom, disappearing from view. When he heard the shower turn on, he let out a slow, controlled breath. This was going to kill him. She had gotten her dress zipped up just fine this morning without help, yet tonight she needed help getting out of it? Not likely. Women knew how to torture men. He would wait right where he was all night if that was what she wanted, but he hoped she'd call for him to join her. He'd told her that she could set the pace, but he wouldn't go too fast, unless he was certain that's what she wanted.

Suddenly a pair of panties and a bra flew through the bathroom doorway to land at his feet. He couldn't resist bending over to pick up the bra. The delicate lace cups were still warm. He wondered what to do next. Was this an invitation? With any other woman, he would have been certain it was, but Celia was different. She might have simply wanted—

"Shall I send you a written invitation?" Celia's voice echoed from the bathroom.

His lips curved up in a wicked grin. Carter let her bra fall back to the floor and started stripping out of his clothes. He nearly tripped in his desperate attempt to get his jeans off. Taking his boots off first probably would have been the smarter move. By the time he stumbled into the bathroom, he had on only a pair of black briefs. The room was already steaming, and he saw only a hint of Celia's body through the opaque shower glass.

He removed his briefs, heart pounding and blood roaring in his ears as he opened the shower door. None of his fantasies over the years could have matched the reality of seeing Celia naked.

"Christ," he muttered, completely at a loss for words.

He marveled at how small and delicate she seemed. She wasn't fragile, but a strong, brave, and loving woman, yet the surge of protectiveness inside him was overwhelming.

Her gaze swept down his body, shyly at first, uncertain, then bolder as she moved back up, lingering on his groin before her lashes fanned up and she met his hungry stare.

He placed his hands on her shoulders and turned her to face away from him so he could massage her tense muscles. She moaned in appreciation. The sound made his body hard, but he kept himself in control. He pushed away a golden lock of wet hair and bent his head to place a tender kiss on her skin between her neck and shoulder. She unfolded her arms from her chest and placed them on the wall to steady herself as he slid an arm around her waist. He could have stared at her forever, memorizing the way her body's curves flowed with the water in an endless waterfall of temptation. He was so close to the thing he wanted most...her. And now he would finally have the chance to take her, to show her how much he adored her without words.

Carter wanted to hold her, to feel their skin connect while the hot water flowed like a river between them. The sacred feeling of holding her, feeling her pulse beneath his lips as he kissed her throat—he wanted it to last forever, yet he felt like he might lose his mind if he had to let her go. She would never know how much he loved her, never know how the beat of his heart was for her and no one else. Celia knew he cared about her, but if she knew just how much...

He pictured himself with her on a bench in a garden, watching the sunset in her eyes as they shared another day together. A life together. A life that would never be. His throat closed as he thought of the children they would never have, sunny-faced phantoms running through the melancholic corners of his mind. The pain of it all threatened to kill the mood, but he turned that pain into resolve. Each time he made love to her, he would honor and cherish her as a tribute to the life he wished they could have together.

Celia turned in his arms and curled her arms around his neck. The mounds of her breasts pressed against his chest, and his breath caught as he saw her eyes, sleepy and seductive. Lust and love burned through him. He wanted to spend hours exploring her body, to find the places that made her shiver and cry out. She tilted her face back, offering her mouth in a bold, unashamed way that he had no intention of resisting.

Their shared breath mingled in the intimate space seconds before they kissed. He took her lips with his own, exploring her as her tongue moved against his in a way that sent bolts of arousal through him. He cupped the back of her head and ravished her mouth, unable to control himself any longer. Celia matched his desire in equal measure, raking the back of his neck with her nails, sending his body into overdrive. It felt as though this was their first kiss and their thousandth, like he had always known how to hold her, how she would feel against him, and how it would fill him with happiness.

They stood beneath the shower spray, mouths fused in that eternal kiss. His hand slid down her back, exploring the slope of her spine and the curve of her bottom. Then he slid one hand up to explore her breasts, feeling the soft globes in his palms, first one and then the other. Her nipples pebbled against his fingertips and he pinched them lightly. Celia in turn slid one hand down his abdomen, grasping his shaft in her small feminine hand and squeezing him. It felt like heaven and for a second he couldn't breathe as she explored him, cupped his balls and pumped her hand slowly up and down him. If this felt too good, he couldn't imagine how being inside her would feel.

Desperate to regain some control, he gently, but firmly faced her away from him and slid a hand down her belly until he found her mound. The tiny bud of her clit peeped out of the folds of her sex and he stroked it reverently, knowing he'd soon have a chance to put his mouth down here, to lick her until she was hoarse from screaming. It felt like he'd waited a damned lifetime to show this woman how much he craved her.

"Oh god, that feels..." she dissolved into a moan as he stroked her folds with one fingertip, exploring her. Then he slid that finger inside her, slow at first, letting her get used to it. She was tight, her sheath gripping him like a fist.

"Do you know how much I've thought about this?" he murmured, nipping her neck as he began to thrust that finger over and over into her, playing with her until she was wriggling her sweet, delectable bottom against his cock.

"How much?" she demanded huskily and the sound of her voice, that deep, that sensual made his body shake.

"Every damn night since I was sixteen. Every fantasy I've ever had...it's always been you." He inserted a second finger now, stretching her a little and he curved his fingers inside her, seeking that g-spot and when he felt it, he rubbed it vigorously, stroking it over and over.

Celia started panting softly "oh shit," over and over again as he thrust his fingers into her.

"That's it, love, tell me how much you can take," he encouraged, loving how much she was breaking apart in his arms, from his touch. He would do everything with her, explore every fantasy because the moment it was over...he'd never be the same. She turned in his arms, breaking free of his fingers and wrapped her arms around his neck kissing him like a woman starved of air.

She pressed tighter against him and broke the kiss to whisper in his ear.

"Here. In the shower. I want you here. Take me hard, make me forget *everything* but you." Her words seemed to echo all around them, bouncing off the tiles. He was never going to forget this moment, how she looked up at him with love drunk eyes and the way she offered him herself, naked emotionally and physically, just like him.

"Thank God," he groaned and backed her up against the wall. He gripped her bottom, lifting her up, and she wrapped her legs around his waist as he pinned her against the wall. Celia clung to his shoulders, and he panted against her neck as he positioned himself at her entrance.

"You're sure?"

She bit her lip and nodded, desire gleaming in her eyes. He teased her entrance, rubbing his shaft along her folds until she wriggled a little and he slid deep into the silky heat between her thighs. Carter lowered her onto his cock, and she hissed out a breath. Her thighs clenched around his hips. Celia was deliciously tight, and he could feel her quake around him as he stretched her with each thrust. Each time he filled her, he wanted to die from the exquisite pleasure. He couldn't stop the need to claim her. He rammed home, his body hard and primal as he rode her.

Celia's head fell back as she breathed raggedly, overwhelmed. They moved together, hands digging into skin, bodies burning with passion. He buried his head against her neck, nipping her throat as he fucked her in a hard, raw rhythm. She was a willing captive to his lust and he to hers. The tension of a pending climax built inside him, but he needed her to come first. He held her tighter against the wall, bracing her weight on one arm while he rubbed the pad of his thumb over her clit until she bucked and cried out his name. He strained, his body and mind fighting the rush that built within him, but then she said the three words that changed his life forever.

"I love you..."

He felt like his body had burst apart like a dying star as he pounded into her, gripping her to him like the precious treasure she was. He felt so connected to her that he couldn't tell where she ended and he began anymore. Carter lifted his gaze to hers.

"I love you too."

It was one thing to live his life knowing he loved her and sensing that she loved him back. But to finally exchange those declarations? To have them confirmed? Validated? Reciprocated? It changed everything. He withdrew from her and set her down on her feet.

"Wow..." Celia wobbled, and he caught her hips, holding herself steady, and she giggled. He laughed as well, feeling so damned good—and scared as hell at the same time. Celia was his, at least for now. Her pleasure-glazed eyes roved over his body in appreciation.

"I was so nervous earlier. I didn't take the time to look at you as much as I wanted," she said.

He had to resist the urge to puff out his chest. "You like what you see?"

"You know you're gorgeous." She laughed, her face red.

"So are you." She was so beautiful it made him hurt inside. She blushed and ducked her head, but he caught her chin and lifted it so she couldn't hide from him.

"No regrets?" he asked.

"No regrets." She curled her arms around his waist, embracing him until reality brought them down from the clouds.

"We should wash and get out before your aunt runs out of hot water."

They reached for the bar of soap on the ledge at the same time. As their fingers brushed, accidentally knocking the soap to the floor, they shared a laugh and he leaned in, kissing her softly in a way that made her heart quiver. He retrieved the bar and handed it to her. She scrubbed herself with the lathery soap, and he did the same. From time to time, they would stop, steal a kiss, brush their hands over each other, and just enjoy the spray of hot water. But they couldn't stay here forever.

Eventually they climbed out. Celia took the fluffy towel Carter offered and shyly covered her body with it. She had no reason to be shy. She had a body built for every one of his fantasies.

She left and returned to her bedroom, probably to change into her pajamas. Carter took a few minutes to take his contacts out and brush his teeth, something he probably should have done prior to the mind-blowing shower sex.

He changed into his pajama pants but didn't bother with a shirt. He was still hot and needed to cool down a little. He had just settled into his bed and put on his glasses when Celia slipped back inside. She wore her blue striped silk pajama shorts and a button-up top. Her towel-dried hair was still a little wet, causing the strands to curl slightly. She would look damn cute tomorrow morning with all those soft waves of gold hair, and he was going to be lying in bed next to her to enjoy it.

With a wink, he threw the covers back to let her in. She bounded over and leapt into bed with a happy grin as she leaned in to kiss his cheek.

"I love your glasses, you know." She stroked a fingertip down the side of his frames. For some reason he got hard from that, like it was some kind of foreplay.

"Oh yeah?" He grasped her hips and forced himself to calm. He wanted to pace himself, and she needed to sleep. They both did if they intended to get any work done tomorrow. As much as he didn't want to work while he was here, he was desperate to send out more pitches about the Pembroke estate to production companies. It would take a miracle, but right now anything seemed possible.

"Yeah. Maybe tomorrow you can wear those while we...you know. It's like you're Clark Kent and Superman."

"I do indeed *know*. And I'm more than happy to play your superhero." It was so bloody adorable how she tried to avoid saying *sex*. She was so shy, yet when she was lost in the heat of the moment, she allowed herself to give in to her desire and was bold and demanding. It was an irresistible combination.

She slid down the bed and cuddled up to him. He turned off the lamp and did the same. He couldn't remember a time when he hadn't loved her. Now the feeling had intensified, because they had shared that last secret part of themselves with each other. The walls of their own personal Jericho had come tumbling down after one hell of a trumpet blast.

He didn't want to think about how he'd have to let her go soon. Maybe, just maybe, he could still find a way to keep her. But in order to do that, he'd have to find some way to help Matthew.

❧ 10 ❧

Celia rubbed her cheek against Carter's chest and let out a contented sigh, aware of the fact that this was the second morning she'd woken in his arms. It felt even better than the first time, no doubt because they'd forged such a powerful connection the night before.

Everything felt different now. The intimacy that they'd shared hadn't just been sex in the shower, but what came after. The soft kisses, the gentle caresses, the caring for each other. She'd become more comfortable with him, so much so that she felt no shyness about moving her hand down his chest toward his pajama bottoms and slipping her fingers under his waistband.

His breathing was still slow and even, and she wondered how long he would stay that way given the proper encouragement. She found his shaft, semierect, and gripped it. He was big, really big, and her thighs quivered at the memory of him driving inside her. It had felt so good, like every erotic dream she'd ever had. But it hadn't been a dream—it had been all too wonderfully real. She was so lost in the memory of last night that she didn't realize she was stroking him until he spoke.

"You're playing with fire, love." Carter's sleep-heavy voice was low and seductive. He opened his eyes, his gaze smoldering.

She continued to stroke his cock. "Then burn me."

His hips jerked, and she tugged his briefs down so his erect shaft sprang free. His body lay before her like a naked god, demanding her worship. She was all too happy to comply. She moved over, and before he could say anything, she took him into her mouth. His breath hitched, and he fisted a hand in her hair. She relished the salty taste of his skin as she briefly released him. He grew harder as she gripped the base of his cock and lowered her head again. She relished the power she now held over him. Celia flattened her tongue underneath his sensitive tip, and he groaned her name. His fingers knotted in her hair. She glanced up, watching his face, loving his reaction. He was so close to coming apart...

Carter pulled her off him, and she moaned a frustrated protest, but he soon silenced her by flipping her onto her back and shoving her pajama top up to expose her breasts. He cupped them, filling his hands, squeezing and caressing them—gently at first, then harder as he buried his face in the valley between them.

She wanted him inside her, and he was controlling himself far too well for her liking. "What are you doing?"

"Torturing you back," he said gruffly. "It's only fair." He tweaked her nipple, and she sucked in a harsh breath as a zing of pleasure shot down to her core. She was aching with need now, the need to have his mouth on her breasts, to have him inside her. He sucked and lapped at each sensitive peak, killing her with exquisite pleasure and torturous restraint.

"Please, Carter. I need you...*now*." She tugged at the gold strands of his hair, urging him to move back up her body. He chuckled in reply and tugged her shorts and panties off.

"Not yet. Not until I've had a taste." He spread her thighs wide, using his shoulders to keep her open. She blushed as he gazed at her most sensitive secret part, as if devising a strategy as to how he would proceed. Then, when he was ready, he unleashed his sensual attack.

He placed light kisses on her inner thighs, then her mound, working his lips down in a heated path to her clit, and she hissed as he sucked on her too sensitive bud. She wasn't going to last, not when he flicked his tongue in and out of her.

"Stop it! Stop teasing me," she begged in a ragged voice. Carter finally slid up her body and grasped her hands in his, lacing their fingers together as he pinned her hands on either side of her head.

He rocked his hips against hers, entering her slowly. Again she went mindless with the sensation of being stretched and filled by him.

Carter caught her mouth with his. She abandoned all her other thoughts and just embraced being with him. When they kissed, it was as though she'd slipped into a secret world, a wooded glen alive with magic, clinging to every mote of dust that drifted between the beams of sunlight. It was their world, one that no one could ever take away from them, even after it ceased to exist and all they had left were their memories.

Celia kissed him harder, desperate to burn his lips into her heart and mind. They came in a mutual shuddering wave of pleasure and love. Carter collapsed on top of her, his lips feathering against her ear as he spoke sweet things she would never share with anyone.

She knew he had been with many women before last night, but now, here, it felt like she had been the only one. In a strange and wonderful way, it felt like this was her first time and his. She stroked her fingers through his hair, brushing it away from his eyes. He breathed slowly now as he laid his head against her breasts. She knew he could feel her heart beating against his cheek.

"I don't know how I can ever let you go after this," he said, his soft voice sounding worried.

She fought a sudden wave of emotion. She didn't want to let go of him either. What would the world be like for her if she had to live the rest of her days pretending she felt this way with someone else?

They didn't say anything for a long while, but finally Carter rolled off her and went to the bathroom. She had a chance to admire his fine muscled ass as he left. When he came back, he had on his pajama bottoms and headed for the door.

She lounged on the bed, still naked from the waist down. "Where are you going?"

"To make you breakfast." He gave her a cocky grin that made her wet all over again.

"Seriously? You've already seduced me quite thoroughly. I don't need waffles too."

He pretended to be disappointed. "No then, to the waffles?"

She threw a pillow at him. He caught it, grinning, and threw it back at her.

"That's a *yes* to the waffles, by the way," she called after him as he left. She collapsed back, stretching her arms above her head and sleepily smiling to herself. What a glorious morning.

Carter soon returned with a tray of food, and she managed to get up and find her knickers and shorts before climbing back into bed. Somehow eating naked in bed just felt wrong. The tray Carter set on her lap had a plate of waffles, fresh butter melting on top, and a small carafe of syrup. There was even a small vase full of fresh wildflowers. She looked from the tray up to him, and the hopeful expression on his face made her heart turn over in her chest.

"It's perfect. *You're* perfect." She reached out to him, and he leaned over, and she kissed him softly. "Go make your own and come join me."

"You sure?"

"Absolutely."

With a chuckle he left, and she took a bite of the waffles, moaning at their crispy, buttery goodness. The man knew how to spoil her.

They shared a quiet breakfast together, smiling at each other and enjoying the simple pleasure of being together, sharing things beyond sex.

They did as Carter had suggested, working a few hours on their laptops before Celia felt satisfied with the progress on her proposal. She saw Carter sigh and send another batch of emails to various production companies and producers. But before he could start on another, she reached over and closed his laptop.

"I think it's time we got some fresh air," she said. "There's only room for one workaholic here, and we both know it's me."

"And I definitely want you working less," he said with a teasing chuckle.

By the time they were ready to go, they ran into Holly in the living room.

"Have a good night last night?" she asked, glancing up from her newspaper. An orange cat that Celia had seen only a few times since arriving was lounging on the couch beside Holly, his tail twitching as he assessed them with an inscrutable feline stare.

"We had a lovely night," Carter said. Then he added with a crooked grin, "Invigorating."

Celia felt a blush rise beneath her skin. *Invigorating.* That was one way to put it. Explosive, glorious, fraught with sexual wildness—those were better ways to describe their night.

"We thought we would do a bit more sightseeing,"

Celia added quickly, hoping to prevent Holly and Carter from starting an innuendo match.

"Carter!" The shrill scream of the parrot overhead made Celia jump. He'd moved to roost on the rafters, it seemed. A second later she realized he had screamed not *Carla* but *Carter*. Had the parrot heard her and Carter last night and this morning? Had her aunt, for that matter?

"Anthony...," Holly warned the parrot in that gentle tone all pet parents used when chastising their pet's behavior.

"We should go." Celia tugged Carter toward the door. "We'll text you if we plan to make it home for dinner."

They barely escaped the house before they burst into laughter. Celia had a suspicion that by the end of their trip, Anthony would know quite a few more colorful phrases.

ৡৢ

THE NEXT TWO WEEKS PASSED IN A BLUR OF ROAD trips, picnics in gold meadows, and dinners at dusk beneath the watchtowers of old Roman and Etruscan cities. They watched the eerie beauty of bats flying at sunset from Volterra, and they admired the precarious-looking tower of Pisa. They spent hours meandering through the art museums of Florence. Carter couldn't remember a time when he'd felt so free, so happy.

Each night he took Celia to bed, and they made love for hours until they crashed into dreamless sleep. Dawn would break over the hills, and he'd have a chance to love her all over again.

But today he was watching Celia's face as she read her emails just after breakfast. Her brows were drawn together.

"My boss wants to have a conference call with

me," she whispered, placing a hand on her stomach as if she felt nauseous.

Carter curled an arm around her shoulders and closed his own computer so he could focus on her. "Why? Did he say?"

"I don't know. He's going to call any minute. What if he wants to fire me?" She buried her face in her hands, not crying, but seeming desolate all the same.

"Why would he fire you? He gave you time to work remotely while here in Italy, didn't he? You felt good about the proposal you turned in, right?"

She nodded, still hiding behind her hands.

"Then there's no need to panic. Go take the call in your room. I'll be right here if you need me." Carter pulled her hands down, and she met his gaze.

"I need this job, Carter. I can't afford to lose it."

"I know." He knew all too well. It wasn't just about the money—it was about one's independence and self-worth. Celia kissed his cheek, her lips trembling against his skin before she picked up her phone and retreated to her room.

Carter opened his computer and read through Tristan's latest email. His usually upbeat best friend who never took no for an answer was frustrated at the responses they'd been receiving from Hollywood. It seemed there was more to playing the game than just having a nice-looking location. There were taxation issues, exclusivity deals, and dozens of other issues he and Tristan were only just discovering. The deeper they got into this, the more it seemed there was to learn.

Carter's heart sank like a stone cast far into a deep, dark lake. He and Tristan needed this, not just because it would free Celia of her promise to marry Callum, but so the estate had a future as a tourist destination.

It was all too easy in England for an estate to lose

income due to the lack of tenant farms, which used to sustain the lands of the landed gentry. In the modern world, the old estates had to find new ways to survive. He and Tristan knew that being attractive to tourists would be key to sustaining Pembroke.

He started a reply email to Tristan, setting out a few changes to their proposal letter, highlighting the estate's proximity to London, the affordable long-term hotels for film crews, and the attributes of the estate and the current staff. He hit send and tried to bury the despair that threatened to choke the last bit of his hope.

The door down the hall opened, and Celia rushed out, tears staining her cheeks.

Oh no...please no...

"Oh my God!" She threw her arms around his neck, hugging him until his lungs burned with the need to breathe.

"What? What happened?"

Laughing, she pulled back to look at him. "Lord Kincade chose me! He loves my proposal and wants me to start right away. We have to go home."

Carter stiffened. They were supposed to have two more weeks of paradise. *Two.* She couldn't take those away from him. He couldn't let her go, not when he'd just glimpsed heaven for the first time. It wasn't fair to have to give her up.

But he had to. She couldn't risk losing this opportunity. And even if it killed him inside, he would support her and do whatever it took to make her happy.

"We're leaving," he echoed, pain numbing every part of him. "Back to London." Back to the rest of his life without this woman. He had known it was going to hurt, but the pain he felt now might just kill him.

"Not London." She brushed her fingers along the back of his neck, confusing his body by starting a war between lust and panic.

"What?" He tried to focus on her words. "Not London?"

She shook her head, her nose wrinkling in adorable exasperation. "Scotland, and you're coming with me. I asked Lord Kincade if it was all right if I brought an assistant, and he said he would like to meet you. He's not much older than us."

"I'm coming with you?" He was so full of forbidden hope that he was afraid to believe it.

"Well, yes. I mean...unless you don't want to?" Celia dropped her arms from his body, a hint of fear in her eyes.

"Of course I bloody want to. I was just worried that..." He choked down the words, fearing they would make him sound like an emotional sap.

She cupped his face, pressing her body close to his. "What?"

"That this"—he waved around them—"was over."

She shook her head, smiling. "It doesn't have to be. Not yet. I was hoping we could spend the next two weeks in Scotland."

"Scotland it is then." He lowered his head, stealing a kiss, tasting the salt of her tears, tears of joy because she'd gotten something she'd worked so hard for. He was thrilled and so damned proud of her. She deserved this moment.

If only I could find a way to make her proud of me in return.

He would do whatever he had to do to make his and Tristan's plans for the Pembroke estate work. He was not going to let Celia go now, not without fighting for her like his life depended on it. She was and always would be his life.

11

Celia sat on the edge of her seat as their private car turned down the long drive toward the Kincade estate. She rolled down the window nearest her, taking in the sweet, piney air that was softened with the aroma of blooming rhododendrons. The castle off in the distance was a rambling thing, but rather than being a dark and forbidding structure, it seemed almost bright in the sunlight because of its smooth stones. The sloping hills around the structure gave way to a loch with waters that reflected the blue summer sky. To the east, there were extensive gardens and a flock of sheep just off the road, a beautiful Scottish collie sitting nearby, eyes locked on his wards. Lord Kincade's castle looked even better in reality that it had in the pictures.

Carter peered out his window. "Now *this* is an estate." He'd have had no trouble getting something filmed here. Everyone in Hollywood loved a good castle.

Celia had to agree with him. She reached for his hand across the seat as she tried to restrain her excitement.

Manor homes were lovely, but there was something primitive and mysterious about a castle. The large, impenetrable stones, the thin slit windows in the towers where men would have fired arrows in the midst of a siege. It was an impressive sight, and she couldn't wait to sink her teeth into the restoration work.

The car stopped at the front steps, and the driver opened Celia's door. Carter got out on his side before the driver could assist him. Celia almost laughed. He would never get used to being waited upon.

The heavy oak doors opened, and a man met them at the bottom of the steps.

"Miss Lynton? Mr. Martin?" he asked in heavy Scottish brogue that was music to Celia's ears. She adored that accent.

Celia met the man on the steps and shook his hand. "Yes, that's us."

"I am Lord Kincade's butler, Mr. Dean. Please, come let me show you to your rooms. Your luggage will be brought up shortly. His lordship will arrive for dinner in two hours. Until then, you are free to explore the grounds as well as the castle's interior." Mr. Dean smiled at Celia warmly. "I understand you are to be in charge of our restoration project, so it would be good for you to familiarize yourself with everything. Let me know if I can be of service to you. My family has been in the employ of the Kincade family for generations."

"Thank you, I appreciate that!" Celia assured him. She sensed Mr. Dean was most proud and protective of the castle. She wondered if Kincade had shown Dean her plans and whether he felt they faithfully kept the castle's beauty intact. Perhaps he had, and that explained the warm welcome.

She and Carter exchanged smiles as they followed Mr. Dean inside. Celia tilted her head back, amazed by the vaulted ceilings and the winding grand stairs that split apart into two hallways on the second floor. She'd seen most of the castle through photographs and had sketched much of it a dozen different ways. But seeing it in person, inhaling the scent of the woods and the gardens, feeling the stones beneath her hands, was something that could only be experienced firsthand.

"This way, please." Mr. Dean motioned for them to follow. The front desk inside the castle's entrance reminded her of a hotel, only more personal. The desk was occupied by a red-haired young man who rushed past them to collect the bags from the car.

"That's Jamie. He'll take care of your suitcases. If you need anything, dial zero on your room phone, and it will connect you to him at the front desk until eight at night. After that, the night staff are here, and a lad named Cory will answer if you need anything. And if you happen to need me, my number is twelve."

Celia let her fingertips trail along the banister. The oak was polished smooth, like silk. The halls on the upper floors were spectacular, portraits lining the walls, with comfortable old leather chairs and over-stuffed couches tucked in alcoves. It was very much a masculine, almost bachelor-like residence. She would keep that in mind what she suggested interior decorators to come in and finish the work after the restorations were complete.

Their rooms, like in Italy, were across the hall from each other. She laughed at Carter's expression when he realized they weren't sharing a room, but it would have been presumptuous of the staff to put them together. She had asked Lord Kincade if she could bring Carter as her assistant because she thought it sounded a little better than her asking to drag a boyfriend along for a free unofficial vacation in Scotland.

"How's your room?" she asked Carter.

He nodded toward his door and shot her a grin. "Come and see."

She slipped past him, and her jaw dropped when

she saw the massive canopy bed with four posts intricately decorated with carved vines worked into the wood. Blue-and-cream brocade curtains laced the canopy and posts. Two leather armchairs faced a large black marble fireplace, completing the look. It was a perfect bedchamber for a man, just as her room with its more delicate wooden painted four-poster and rose-red hangings was better suited for a lady.

"Reminds me a bit of Pembroke, really," Carter said. Celia leaned against his side, hugging him. She loved how much he adored her uncle's estate. He saw it as his home because he'd grown up there. But that was part of British culture. People who worked on these vast estates weren't simply servants—they had a right to call these estates their home, because they were part of the system that kept these places afloat, both through thin days and times of plenty. Men and women like Carter were vital to the survival of such places. It made him incredibly valuable, yet Celia knew he didn't recognize his own worth.

"Your father still handling everything okay?" she asked.

Carter kissed the top of her head and squeezed her waist. "He's well enough. I imagine he'll be glad to have me home in a couple of weeks." His tone took on a hint of melancholy, one she understood because she felt the same. Only two more weeks together, and then it would all be over. She would announce her engagement to Callum, and...

Celia shut down that train of thought before it could leave the station.

Carter pulled her in front of him and cupped her face, kissing her gently. The sort of kiss that made her want to curl up in his arms by a warm fire while it snowed outside.

"Want to test out the bed?" he murmured against her lips.

She shivered and placed her hands on his chest.

His muscles leapt beneath her palms, and his eyes burned with hunger. She started walking back toward the bed and pulled him along by the shirt. "Maybe…"

When they reached the bed, he caught her by the waist and lifted her up. She wrapped her jean-clad legs around his waist, and he leaned over her, his lips capturing hers, this time with raw, wild lust that sent her senses spinning. As she gripped his shirt and pulled it over his head, someone knocked on the door.

"Damn it all," Carter growled adorably against her mouth. She teased him by running a hand down his chest to his groin, cupping him through his jeans. He moaned helplessly.

He started to kiss her again. "Maybe they will go away."

There was another knock, and Mr. Dean spoke through the closed door.

"Mr. Martin. Miss Lynton. His lordship has arrived early and has asked me to invite you both to join him in the library."

"Thank you, Mr. Dean," Celia said as Carter worked his hands under her shirt to cup her breasts, and then she bit her lip to stifle a giggle at the compromising situation they were in. When they were sure he was gone, Carter kissed her again, this time with a desperation born of knowing they couldn't do anything else right now.

"Soon," he promised.

"Soon," she agreed. She immediately missed him as he let go and stepped back from her.

She handed him back his shirt, and she ran her fingers through her hair before they headed downstairs. They found Mr. Dean waiting at the foot of the stairs. There was a soft twinkle in his eyes, as though he knew exactly what he'd interrupted.

"His lordship is this way." Dean led them to a large library that made Celia's heart leap.

Books filled the room, tucked in all the nooks and crannies of the shelves, filling every available space. A book lover. Celia recognized a kindred spirit instantly and smiled.

A man stood at the long table in the center of the room, his hands pressed flat on the stout oak table as he studied some architectural plans laid out before him. He raised his head as Mr. Dean escorted Celia and Carter inside. Kincade was a tall, muscled man, and he was wearing a white dress shirt and gray trousers. And he was handsome—she could certainly admit that—with dark hair and gray eyes, but her tastes ran toward fair hair. She wanted to reach for Carter's hand but didn't. It would be unprofessional.

"Miss Lynton." Lord Kincade glanced between her and Carter. "And Mr. Martin?" He skirted the desk and came over to shake their hands.

"It's a pleasure, my lord," Celia said, and Carter echoed her words.

"Please, it's Garrick. I insist."

"You have an astounding library, Garrick," said Carter. His gaze roved around the tall shelves and the gleaming spines illuminated by sunlight from the high windows.

Garrick looked upon the bookcases with pride. "Thank you. My family has always been obsessed with books. When the castle partially burned down in 1821, my ancestor Brock Kincade and his English wife, Joanna, filled the new library with hundreds of books. Many of them are at least a century or two old. It's hard not to appreciate their obsession."

"A noble obsession," Celia said.

"I like to think so. Now, to business." Garrick turned back to the table of plans. Celia rather liked that he brushed aside niceties and pretenses to focus instead on work. As they joined him at the table, Celia had a sudden flutter in her stomach. She realized Carter would be watching her work on her first big project. No pressure there. She focused on the plans and began to walk Garrick through the renovations, hoping she could pull this off like the professional she believed herself to be.

⚜

CARTER COULD WATCH CELIA TALK FOR HOURS. SHE was completely engaged in her vision, and Garrick seemed spellbound by it as well.

He loves his home as much as I love Pembroke.

His cell phone vibrated in his pocket. He murmured his excuses as he left the library to check on it. It was a voicemail from Tristan.

"Carter, don't panic, but your father's in the hospital. He had a minor heart episode. I'm with him and so is Father. Call me when you can."

Carter gripped his phone so tightly it felt like his fingers would break. Hospital? He tried to steady his breathing and calm the rush of his thoughts as he dialed Tristan back. It was his worst fear, to be away from home when his only parent needed him most.

Tristan answered on the second ring. "Carter, thank God."

"How is he?" The words scraped out of his throat.

"Fine for now. His vitals are good but they are running some tests, but. It seems his heart was out of rhythm, which happens to men at his age, according to the medic."

"Can I speak with him?" Carter asked.

"I'd say yes, but he's asleep. I can call you back when he's awake."

"Yes, please." Carter paused and spoke again. "Tristan, should I come home?"

Tristan sighed. "Let me talk to the medics. I know you don't have much time left with Celia, and I wouldn't want to take that from you."

Carter pressed his thumb and forefinger against

his closed eyes and drew in a deep breath. It didn't help ease the tightness in his chest. "I know."

"Breathe," Tristan told him, and Carter nearly smiled.

"I just did."

"Keep doing it. I know you. When you're worried, you forget the little things like oxygen."

"You're such an ass," Carter growled, but he was smiling now. Tristan always knew how to cut the tension. It reassured him somehow that his father was going to be okay.

"I'm hanging up now," Tristan warned with a chuckle. "Go to Celia. I'll call you as soon as your father is up and let you know what the doctors say. And to make sure you're still breathing."

"Thank you." Carter slipped his phone back in his trouser pocket. He scrubbed a hand over his face as he considered what to do.

In the end, there was only one thing to be done. He would leave in the morning. Back inside the library, he was glad to see that Celia was still fully invested in her presentation. She had worked so hard on this project, and he was so proud of her. By the way Kincade was listening to her, he seemed to be in agreement with her approach. Lord, the woman was brilliant and talented.

"Excellent. I can have the work hired out immediately," Kincade said as he rolled up the architectural plans and put them away inside a gray plastic tube.

"Carter, Mr. Kincade is going to give us a tour of the house and grounds before dinner." Celia beamed at him, and it almost banished the shadows growing inside him. He couldn't tell her about his father, not right now.

He held out his hand, and she took it. He squeezed her fingers gently, the contact grounding him so he didn't feel like his panic would resurface and drown him. They followed Kincade to the front drive, the white stone gravel crunching beneath their feet as Kinkade talked about his home.

"This is part of the original castle, dating back to the fifteenth century..."

Carter barely paid attention to the tour, watching instead the way the wind tugged on Celia's hair and how her eyes sparkled with wonder as she brushed her hands over the thick, heady-scented blossoms of overgrown rhododendrons that lined the sides of the drive. She belonged on a vast estate like this, among centuries-old stones and ancient family portraits.

Carter couldn't offer her a future that would give her any of that, not even if all of Hollywood came clamoring at his door. He'd always known that, but it had never stopped him from loving her. Maybe it was time to let her go. Perhaps his father's attack was a sign. He couldn't win this fight, and another two weeks would only make things worse.

He let go of her hand as she rushed to speak with a groundskeeper about the manicured garden. Kincade drifted back until the men were side by side.

"So, how long have you and Miss Lynton been together?" he asked, meeting Carter's surprised gaze.

"We haven't... We aren't..." Although, he'd been playing the part of an assistant, but it seemed Garrick had seen right through that.

"Because I heard from a friend that she's been seen with Callum Radcliffe. Rather *officially* seen, if you follow me. Rumor has it an announcement isn't far off."

Carter shoved his hands in his pockets and shrugged, trying to figure out what he could say.

"I know Callum—I know him very well. Well enough that I'm guessing something rather unthinkable. It's merely for show, isn't it?"

Carter finally met Kincade's gaze again, expecting judgment or disapproval, but he saw only compassion and understanding from a man who was a stranger to him.

"I've loved her since we were children," he confessed. "Since before a boy even knows what love really is." The words sounded foolish to his ears, but they were true, and he refused to be ashamed of them.

"The rumor is that she's engaged to Callum...what happened?"

"Her family lost everything and had to be rescued by her uncle."

"Lord Pembroke," Kincade said matter-of-factly.

Carter nodded. "Celia's brother, Matthew, has been diagnosed with autism and severe dyslexia. He got into a fight in Eton with some boys who bullied him and was asked to leave. He's been accepted to Ravenswood which has a focused program for math and science, but they don't take financial aid from the National Health Service. Celia is doing her best to provide for him and the expensive tuition they'll need to pay."

"And Callum?"

Carter didn't feel comfortable revealing too much. "They have an understanding," he said. "It's a mutually beneficial arrangement."

"I see."

Kincade and Carter walked farther down the path, not speaking for a time.

"But you would provide for her if you could?" Kincade asked.

Carter smiled wryly. "I'd give my life, but she needs money, and that's the one thing I don't have. I've been desperately trying to make things work. Lord Pembroke's son, Tristan, and I have been pitching the estate as a filming location. We want it to be like Highclere was for *Downton Abbey*."

"But you've had no luck?"

"None. There are dozens of other places to film

aside from our estate. The competition is fierce. I don't know what else to do. Celia needs me, and I'm powerless to help her." He raked a hand through his hair as they entered the gardens. Ahead of them, Celia was still talking to the groundskeeper.

"I understand that all too well," Kincade said, his gaze solemn and his face reflected an unspoken pain of his own.

"I'm afraid I have to leave early tomorrow morning. My father is in the hospital. I don't want to tell Celia tonight. She'll only worry, and I want her to be happy so she keeps focused on this project. She's worked so hard for this." Carter wanted Kincade to see Celia's value, to see her work and respect her for it as any man should.

"To be honest, she presented the only project that I could consider. She understood that I didn't want the castle changed, only improved and modernized where necessary. All the other proposals were unacceptable."

"Would you tell her boss that? She's new to the firm, and they aren't paying her nearly what she's worth."

Surprise colored Kincade's eyes. "Is that so? Yes, I absolutely will put in a call to Mr. Ridings."

"Thank you." Carter continued to watch Celia, his heart tightening as though invisible bands of steel were crushing it bit by bit.

Tonight would be his last night with her. He would have to make it count.

12

Something was wrong. Celia kept looking at Carter across the dinner table, but he was avoiding her gaze. Even when she spoke to him, he would respond briefly and then return the conversation back to Garrick. Carter was smiling and talking, perfectly charming as always, but when he thought no one was watching, he changed. A shadow flashed across his face, and sorrow deepened his eyes. It followed him, barely visible under the surface, through the conversations at dinner and the brandy they shared in the library with Garrick afterward.

Was he thinking about them returning to London? Why? They still had fourteen more days. But his mood made her feel as though she was watching each grain of sand in their invisible hourglass drop, a constant reminder of what would happen on the last day.

She and Carter bid Garrick good night and returned to their rooms. Carter paused at the doorway, his back to her, and she could see the tension in his lean, strong form. She drew closer to him, wishing that neither of them was thinking about when all this would end. But that wasn't what he needed. She pressed a hand to his shoulder.

"Carter. What is it?"

He grasped her face in his hands and slanted his

mouth over hers in a wild, desperate kiss. It stung with a bittersweet ache, a kiss that warned of good-byes and cold beds. Her throat tightened, and she closed her eyes, fighting off a rush of tears. She curled her arms around his neck as he pushed the door behind him open and carried her into his room. He pushed her back against the closed bedroom door as he kissed her deeply, delving between her lips.

Hunger spiraled through her, and she reached for his trousers, unfastening the belt and unzipping him. He groaned against her as she slipped her hand inside.

"I need you," she whispered, stroking him. "Please, Carter."

He stole another heady kiss from her and let her go, turning her body so she faced the heavy wooden door.

"Hands on the wall."

Celia placed her palms on the ancient oak and gasped as he shoved her skirt up to her waist and tugged her panties down to her knees.

"Spread for me." Carter's low growl was so intense she swore her entire body would catch fire. She had never seen this side of him—dominating, aggressive, commanding. She had never been with a man like that before, but Lord, she liked it. Liked him. He was reduced down to animal instincts and need, and a woman liked to know when she made a man lose control like that.

Carter's mouth caressed her neck as he brushed her hair back over one shoulder. She shivered as he stroked a hand over her bare ass before he gave it a playful slap. They shared a moan as he nudged her folds with the head of his shaft.

"Ready for me?" he asked in a dark whisper.

She managed to nod, and he rammed in hard. The fullness of him inside her, their connection so deep and overwhelming, all of it made her pant. He took her slow, hard, owning her with every thrust as she dug her nails into the wood.

No words were needed. They didn't need to pretend in this moment that they were civilized. This was raw passion, pure and simple. When she came, her vision was blanketed with an explosion of stars. He shouted her name, and she felt his release inside her. With a pang of sorrow, she wished for a moment she wasn't on birth control. She wanted his child, not Callum's.

"You okay, love?" Carter asked as he withdrew from her. She turned on shaky legs, kicking off her panties and fixing her skirt. She wasn't going anywhere but his bed tonight. Whatever shadows had darkened his eyes over dinner, she wanted to erase them between the sheets with the passion that burned between them.

"I'm wonderful." She reached for the zipper on her dress and tugged it down. Then she let the dress fall to the floor. He leaned back against the bed's mattress as he removed his shirt and then opened his arms to her.

They fell back into bed, cuddling close between the sheets and kissing. It was the sort of lazy, seductive making out she'd always wanted to have with a man, one that followed an intense amount of sex. Lord, the man knew how to kiss as though that was the only thing that mattered. He fisted one hand in her hair at the nape of her neck and rolled her beneath him so he could fully capture her lips. She raked her nails lightly along his back, rocking her hips up against his and surrendered to him in every way. This man was her dream, the life she'd always wanted and right now she was desperate to pretend that they had forever to be just like this.

She wasn't sure how many times they made love that night. Five? Six? By the end she was so exhausted she didn't think she could come again, but he managed to coax one last sweet, lingering, rippling climax out of her. Now she lay in his arms, not caring that the floor was littered with their clothes and the smell of sex filled the air, mixed with those of the garden from the partially open windows. Carter was still awake, tracing patterns on her back with one hand. The world outside had faded to a dim memory, and she let this single moment become a cocoon for them. Whenever she touched him, her heart seemed to be surrounded by a blaze of light and love that could fight any darkness that came her way.

She could picture the future with him in her mind's eye. A quiet life in a small, cozy cottage on the Pembroke estate. The smell of roasted coffee in the morning, the rustle of newspapers as they shared muffins and marmalade. And someday a baby in a cradle, with lovely eyes and a toothless smile as it reached for them with tiny little hands.

And someday, that child would race through the meadows just as they had done as children. She would curl her arm through Carter's as they took an evening stroll together, his hair and hers streaked with gray, while she looked back on their years together and found that she had been deliriously happy, never wanting anything or anyone but him.

And cruelly, she was reminded that that future, the one she wanted more than anything, was the one she could never have. She couldn't stop the flood of tears that followed, nor the sobs that shook her body. It wasn't fair. None of this was.

"Celia?" Carter's arms tightened around her. "What's the matter?"

"I...don't want this to end." It was all she could say. If she dared say more, it would crush her.

He shushed her, pressing his lips to hers in a burning, tender kiss that seemed to go on forever. "I don't either."

She would always remember him this way—

strong, beautiful, loving, and full of passion. It would have to be enough to get her through the days to come.

***

Carter slipped out of bed a few hours before dawn and dressed. He turned to look at Celia asleep, her hair spread out across the pillows in waves of muted gold. Her limbs were partially entwined in the blankets, and he caught a glimpse of a bare calf, a peek of a delicate elbow. He would never see this again, and it crushed him, broke his soul apart like waves against a rocky shore. But it was the right thing to do. Make a clean break. If he didn't go now, he'd never be able to leave.

He leaned over the bed and kissed her lightly on the forehead, then set the folded note on the empty pillow beside her. He retrieved his suitcase and slipped out of the room.

Mr. Dean was downstairs, waiting for him.

"The cab is waiting. It will take you to Edinburgh and from there a train back to London. Are you certain you don't wish to use Lord Kincade's plane? He is happy to offer it to you."

"No, thank you, Mr. Dean. The train is fine." The train was all he could afford. He knew Kincade wouldn't charge him for the plane, but it was the principal of the matter, just like Italy. He didn't want to feel like he owed anyone.

"Very well, sir." Mr. Dean escorted him to the cab. Carter leaned out of the passenger side of the cab and took one last look at the towering stones of Castle Kincade, then shut the door.

He reached Edinburgh and boarded his train. A number of long-distance commuters and travelers joined him on his car from the towns and cities along the way. With each mile, he moved farther and farther from the woman who owned his heart. It became harder for him to breathe. She would be waking up soon, reaching for him in bed and finding...nothing. Just a note. It would hurt her, being left alone after everything they'd shared. He knew that because he was feeling cut open himself. She deserved a goodbye face-to-face, but that would have been just too hard for him.

I'm a bastard, but if I'd stayed, it would only have delayed the inevitable.

He'd never wanted to hurt Celia, but this was the one hurt he'd known was be unavoidable. He had to leave her in Scotland where her future lay. He wouldn't let her jeopardize her career because his father was ill.

Carter watched the endless cycle of people boarding and disembarking over and over. A cold numbness slithered through him, stealing the last vestiges of joy left inside him. By the time the train reached London several hours later, that feeling had become his constant companion.

He went straight to Tristan's flat and left his suitcase in the spare bedroom before heading to the hospital. He found Tristan and Kat waiting outside his father's hospital room.

"Carter! You're here!" Tristan leapt up from his chair and hugged him tight before letting him go to allow Kat to do the same.

"How is he?" Carter asked.

"Good. The doctors are running some tests," said Kat. "If the results are good they think he can go home by this evening."

As if on cue, a doctor and nurse left, giving them a nod. "We're done for now. You can go in. The results are good and we can release him today."

"Thank you, doctor."

"But," The doctor hesitated, meeting Carter's gaze. "His stress levels are too high for a man his age. I recommend he relaxes more, perhaps he could go on a holiday before returning for work."

"I think we can manage that," Carter said. He'd known he would soon be taking over for his father and now seemed like a the perfect time.

"Good, forced rest is difficult, but he will be better for it."

Carter thanked the doctor. Inside the room, his father was propped up in his bed with a number of pillows behind him. He looked frail and weak. Carter was used to seeing his father as a strong, fit robust presence, a man who had slightly windburned cheeks from touring the grounds daily with the groundskeeper at the estate and a merry twinkle in his eyes behind his silver wire-rimmed glassless. But now his father's face was pale, and the glint in his eyes were slightly dimmed.

Carter swallowed hard. "Father." He was careful as he embraced his father, like he was made of glass.

"Carter, what are you doing here? You had another two weeks in Italy, didn't you? I hope you didn't come home because of me."

Carter nodded, his heart clenching. "It's all right. It was time to come home."

"Son..." Somehow that single word was filled with understanding. Carter swallowed thickly and faced the window in the room, looking out over the London streets below, wishing he could stop feeling altogether. He looked back and forced a smile on his face.

"So, you're coming home tonight?"

His father nodded. "The doctor said I need to focus on relaxing more. He recommended I go on a holiday. Can you imagine? Leaving the estate? Not possible. There'd be too many things to handle while I'm gone." His father said this with his usual bluster and pride. He did love his job, but it had taken a grave toll on him over the years.

"You should go, Father. Speak to Lord Pembroke about it."

"Speak to me about what?" Lord Pembroke asked as he walked into the room. He smiled as he saw Carter. "Glad to see you home, Carter. How was Italy?"

"Good, my lord," Carter replied carefully, not wanting to remind his lordship that he'd been sleeping with the man's niece.

"Well, John, are you ready? I've spoken to the doctor, and they agreed to let you leave now if you feel up to it."

"Yes. I suppose I do," John said.

"My lord," Carter said. The earl turned to him. "The doctor recommended my father take a break from his duties and go on holiday. Would that be possible? I would be willing to take over his work immediately."

"And I'll be helping as well, Father," Tristan added.

"Carter," John admonished him. He turned toward Pembroke. "Don't listen to him. I'm quite fine. I'd go mad if I had to spend a few weeks sitting about."

The earl frowned at John, then looked to Carter. "The doctor recommended it?"

"Strongly," Carter replied at the same time his father protested.

"Hush, John. If the doctor recommends it, by God you'll do it. Full paid leave for a month. End of discussion. I have some friends in Wales who run one of those bed-and-breakfasts on their estate. You'll like it. They have an excellent river. I'll call them tomorrow. You and I can go fly-fishing, lord knows I haven't done enough fishing lately."

John's eyes widened. "You'll come with me?"

The earl chuckled, a rare thing. "Of course. If I'm

not there to watch over you, you'll try to be the steward of that estate too. Besides, our sons have a handle on things?"

Carter nodded in open relief. If his father would listen to anyone, it was Lord Pembroke.

"It's settled, then. We'll let you rest a few days at home, and then we're off to Wales."

"Fly-fishing," Carter's father said with a sigh like a young boy.

Carter smiled. He hadn't seen his father so relaxed in a long time. It reminded him that it was time for him to take over for his father. Permanently. Time to leave his foolish dreams behind and take his place as steward. He stepped out into the hall and found Tristan waiting for him.

"Where's Kat?" he asked.

"Fetching some coffee." Tristan had his hands on his hips. "What happened?"

"What do you mean?"

"Celia. Where is she?" Tristan's eyes searched Carter's face for answers. They'd been friends their entire lives. Sometimes it felt as though they were brothers. They'd shared so much, but he didn't want to share his pain with Tristan.

Carter slipped his hands into his pockets and leaned against the wall. "She's in Scotland."

"Scotland? What happened to Italy?"

"We were there until two days ago. She was selected to help restore a Scottish castle, and the owner flew us to Edinburgh."

"Who's that now?"

"Lord Kincade."

"Oh? Garrick?" Tristan smiled. "Nice bloke. Had a rough time of it. His wife died last year, you know. Cancer. He's been hiding away in his home ever since, from what I hear."

"I didn't know about his wife." Carter remembered the quiet, brooding intensity of the man, which now spoke volumes.

"Why didn't Celia come back with you?" Tristan asked.

"I left while she was asleep. She'd want to come, but she needs to stay in Scotland and finish her work. It could make her reputation in the firm. That's what matters."

Tristan shook his head. "You bloody fool. You'll only upset the poor girl."

Carter sighed. "I know, but what choice did I have? We were getting too close. The longer we were together, the harder it was going to be to say good-bye. I needed to cut it off cleanly before it was too late."

Tristan laid a hand on his shoulder. "When I broke up with Kat, it almost killed me." Tristan's eyes grew distant. Carter knew he was reliving that pain. But he'd been lucky—he'd fought to be with Kat, and they'd been together ever since. But Carter didn't have that luxury.

"What will you do now?" Tristan asked.

Carter shrugged. "Well, it seems our fathers are leaving for Wales to do a month of fishing. You and I are in charge of the estate while they're gone."

"So burying your broken heart in work?" Tristan guessed. "How very English of you."

Carter didn't respond, though that was exactly what he planned to do. Bury himself so deep in work that he'd never have a chance to think of Celia and the joy she'd given him. He closed his eyes, trying to stay calm, or else he'd breakdown right there in the hospital hallway.

"Well, let's get your father home first. Then I say we drink ourselves under the nearest table with my father's best Scotch whisky. The stash he thinks I don't know about."

"Finally, something I'd want to do," Carter said

wryly. But there weren't enough bottles of scotch in the world to drown out the pain he felt.

***

CELIA AWOKE TO AN EMPTY BED, HER HAND reaching for the hard masculine body that wasn't there anymore. Her fingertips brushed over a piece of paper, and she rolled over, holding it up in the morning light.

CELIA,

I'm sorry I couldn't stay. My father is in the hospital, and I have to go to him. We both knew saying goodbye would be hard, and I didn't want to make this any more difficult than it had to be. We both have our families to think about. I'll never forget a single moment of our time together. I will always belong to you.

Yours forever,
Carter

THE LETTER ENDED SO ABRUPTLY THAT CELIA READ it several times, trying to will more words onto the page. Tears welled up in her eyes, and she folded the note, setting it on the nightstand with a shaky hand.

Fourteen days. Those precious moments with him had been stolen, and he wanted to make it sound like he'd done her a *favor*? She stayed in bed for over two hours, unable to move. Her thoughts ran like quicksilver, flowing too quickly for her to grasp or make sense of except for the agony building inside her chest.

Only after Mr. Dean knocked at the door did she finally find the strength to move.

"Miss Lynton? You didn't come down to break-fast. His lordship was worried…"

She cleared her throat of the sob she'd trapped there. "I'm…not feeling well. Please tell Lord Kincade I'm sorry for being late. I'll be down in an hour."

"Very good, miss." Mr. Dean's footsteps receded as he left.

Celia slipped out of bed and walked into Carter's bathroom. His scent still hung in the air like a ghost, teasing her with memories of whispered words, hands roaming over her body, and unions deep in the night that had left her feeling a bliss unlike anything she'd ever experienced before.

It was one thing to know that she loved him—she'd always known that. But the last two weeks had allowed her to catch a glimpse of what their life together could have been, was soul shattering.

She knew that she shouldn't have to pay for her parents' mistakes. But then, life wasn't fair. She'd been raised knowing that truth above all others.

She showered and dressed, unable to summon any energy except what she needed to function. Even the beautiful castle couldn't shake her from the bleakness that curled around her heart, slowly suffocating her. Garrick was waiting for her in the library, a tray of tea and biscuits sitting untouched on the table beside the architectural plans. When he saw her, his smile faltered.

"Celia, Mr. Dean said you were feeling unwell." He walked around the table and put a hand on her shoulder. "Are you all right?"

"I'm fine," she lied.

Garrick was quiet a long moment, studying her anxiously. He released her shoulder. "I'm sorry Mr. Martin had to leave," he said. "I understand you two were very close."

Celia nodded as she stepped up to the table with

the plans. She had to focus on her work, not on the man who'd left her brokenhearted.

"We...we should look into the electrical systems in the new bedrooms here. They will need to be rewired once we restore the wall paneling." She pointed to that section of the plans, her hands visibly shaking.

Garrick clasped her hand in his. "If there's one thing I've learned in life it's that you cannot let *any-thing* stand between you and the person you love. Carter mentioned your troubles regarding your brother. The school and tuition. If that problem didn't exist, would you spend the rest of your life with him?"

There was a lump in her throat. She was mortified that Carter had shared her personal issues with Garrick, but at the same time it was a relief to talk about it. She nodded.

"Then heed my advice. Go after Carter and ask him to marry you. Now. You will find another way to pay for Matthew's school. Trust me."

"But—"

Garrick's eyes hinted at a deep buried pain as he stared down at her. "Turning away from love? That will haunt you forever. If you lose love because you were afraid, you will have only half a life, Celia."

"But I made a promise. Callum also has..." She didn't know how to explain his delicate situation, but Garrick smiled.

"I know about Callum. Or rather, I suspect. He's a good man, and he should not have to hide from love any more than you should. No matter what others think."

"But what about the proposal for the castle? I can't leave now."

Garrick waved a hand dismissively. "I have more than enough to work with for now. You can come back in a few weeks. I'll call Mr. Ridings and tell him how pleased I am with the work so far. You have nothing to worry about."

Celia's heart pounded as she realized that she could do it—she *could* go after Carter and risk everything.

"Why?" She barely knew Garrick, and yet he was counseling her in the most important moment of her life.

Garrick smiled. "Because I couldn't have my happy ending. My wife died two days after we got married at the hospital. The end came so fast, I..." He paused, his voice roughening. "I didn't even have time to take her on a honeymoon. I would give anything to change that, but I can't. I can, however, allow others to not miss out on their chance. Carter is as madly in love with you as you are with him. I can't stand by and let you ruin your lives."

"How do I know if he..." She held her breath, trying to find the words. "Wants me enough to fight for what we have? What if it's just me who feels this way? I can't just go back to London and make a fool of myself if he doesn't feel the same."

Garrick caught her chin and lifted her face up. "Of course you can. That man would give anything for you, and unfortunately, he's convinced himself that what he needs to do is to let you go. Prove him wrong."

Prove him wrong. Celia squared her shoulders. She could do that. Let go of her fear. Let go of what everyone expected her to do and do what she *wanted* to do. She could do it. She could convince Carter that they'd figure out everything else somehow.

Celia threw her arms around Garrick, hugging him. "Thank you."

"Go. My plane is at the airport. You can take it straight to London."

She hugged him again before she raced upstairs to

pack. By the time she was ready, Mr. Dean had a car waiting for her.

She wasn't going to think about the risks; she was going after the man she loved. She was going to convince him they could make this work. Love could find a way.

"I'm coming, Carter."

13

As the car turned into the drive of the Pembroke estate, Celia clenched her shaking hands together. She was going to find Carter and tell him she wasn't marrying Callum. Then she was going to kiss him, make him forget why he'd ever left her, and only then, when he was good and seduced by her kiss, would she tell him that they could make this work. They'd find a way. Whatever it took, she would do it. He was worth it. *They* were worth it.

The driver stopped in front of the main entrance and retrieved her suitcase from the boot while she pressed on the doorbell, her heart racing. At her uncle's house, she'd always felt a bit like a guest. But this was Carter's home, too, and always had been.

Her mind was awash with ideas and complications that still needed to be ironed out. They'd have to save every penny from work, and she could get a second job at night and on the weekends. They could use Tristan's flat in London while they scraped together enough for Matthew's tuition. Wait, no—Carter had to run the estate. They'd have to have a long-distance relationship until she could find a way to work from the estate and not be in London five days a week. Maybe she could ask her uncle if they could stay in one of the hunting lodges during the holidays...

The door opened and shook her out of her thoughts. She'd expected the butler to answer, but instead she found herself facing her uncle.

"Celia?" Uncle Edward looked her up and down in surprise. "I thought you were still in Scotland. Are you all right?" He waved for her to come inside.

"I was..." She glanced around. "How is Mr. Martin?"

"He's resting upstairs. We brought him home only a few hours ago."

"Thank goodness. When Carter left, I was so worried. Where is he?" She hoped her uncle wouldn't be upset, but he likely knew they'd spent the past two of weeks together. Carter hadn't been able to keep that from him when he'd asked for his holiday leave.

"I believe he is taking a walk in the grounds to clear his head. Seeing John in the hospital was hard on all of us, but him especially."

"Then I'll just go—"

Her uncle caught her arm gently, stopping her. "Celia, the boy needs time to clear his head after seeing his father and I believe it's time we had a talk." He nodded toward the open door of his study. She was afraid of what he might know about her and Carter, but she couldn't say no. He was letting her family live in a cottage on the grounds. If he wanted to lecture her, she would have to listen—she owed him that much. But he wasn't going to change her mind, not when it came to who she loved or who she married.

She followed him to the study and sat down opposite him after he eased into the leather chair behind his desk. She took the silence that followed as a cue to speak first.

"Uncle—"

He raised a hand to silence her. "Celia, do you know what's expected of you?"

With a tight throat she nodded. "To marry well,

to increase the family's social connections, to be a good wife and mother."

"Those are your parents' expectations." He steepled his fingers, his gaze downcast. "But they are no longer mine. Times are changing. I admit I've been too old-fashioned, too set in my ways. Trapped in the past, you might say. After I almost lost Tristan, I finally changed too."

Celia stared at her uncle. For years he had been the stern voice in her family, demanding duty before love, and family before anyone else. She didn't know what to say. She hadn't expected to hear him say this. She had expected to have to defy him, battle against everything he stood for, but he wasn't telling her to marry for family and duty.

"Uncle, I don't understand..."

"Do you love him? Carter, I mean, not Radcliffe."

She nodded.

"And would you give up everything to spend your life with him? Your parents, your home, your social standing...Matthew's place at Ravenswood Academy?" Edward asked.

She tilted her head, realizing for the first time that her uncle had known all along what she was planning. She shouldn't have been surprised.

"So you know that Callum and I had agreed to a marriage of convenience for Matthew's sake?"

"Of course. There's nothing I don't eventually find out about around here. Now, would you give it all up for Carter?"

"Yes." The word came out steady, despite her body vibrating with panic. Why was he asking her this?

"You won't have any regrets?"

She didn't answer right away, not because she felt she would have any regrets, but because she wanted him to understand she'd thought this through—all of it.

"My only regret would be to live without him. We'll find a way to help Matthew." She had thought of nothing else since Garrick had spoken to her. She had been building toward this moment her whole life; she just didn't know it until then. She'd only needed to spend a few weeks with Carter, just the two of them, to know for certain that he was the love of her life, and she couldn't sell her happiness, or his, for anything.

Finding true love in a world like this was rare, far too rare. And she had been attempting to reject the gift the universe had given her. Her eyes were finally open. Waking alone with only the memories of the joy she'd experienced with Carter had shown her what the rest of her life would be without him, and she wasn't going to let that happen.

I will fight the whole world just for the chance to love him.

"If that is your desire, then I give you my blessing."

For a second her uncle's words didn't register.

"What?" She needed to hear him repeat the words.

"My blessing to marry him, Celia. You have it." Her uncle's eyes twinkled, and his usual stern expression had vanished.

She smiled, though she was stunned that he was approving the match. "Isn't it the man who usually asks for the blessing?"

Her uncle laughed. "We both know that he's too noble-hearted to ask you to marry him. I fear you'll have to be a modern woman and be the one who proposes. Queen Victoria proposed to Albert over a hundred years ago, I think you can do it." Edward chuckled and stood, and Celia followed suit. Her heart felt light, and hope began to blossom like a budding flower inside her.

"Uncle...why are you allowing this? I know Tristan's accident was a shock to everyone..."

Edward was silent for a moment. Then he looked beyond her, out the window toward the gardens.

"I once loved someone very much. Someone considered unsuitable to my position. Things were different then, she and I...we were soulmates. I know that sounds rather silly, but it fit. When I was with her, I felt there was nothing I couldn't do. But...to my eternal shame, I didn't fight for her. Instead, I stood by as best man and watched her marry my dear friend. And later, when she grew ill and I watched her fade away, I didn't even have the right to grieve for her as a husband, or as a lover. Those regrets follow you to your grave. I wouldn't wish that pain upon anyone else, certainly not you."

"Carter's mother," Celia whispered. "You did love her, didn't you?"

Edward smiled, though it was tinged with sadness. "More than my own life." He looked away for a moment, trying to compose himself. "When I look at that boy, all I see is her. And she would have wanted him to have the world at his feet. And you, my dear, are Carter's world. From the moment you met as children, it was so plain for the world to see that you belonged together. I won't stand in the way of that, as long as I know you'll do everything to be with him, to make each other happy."

"I will, Uncle. I promise."

"Good, good. Well, you'd best go find him."

"Thank you, Uncle Edward." She hugged him and rushed to the door that led to the main grounds. The setting sun, ruby-red, kissed the tops of the trees on the horizon. Celia studied the gardens and the entrance to the woods beyond, catching a glimpse of Carter walking into the fields between the gardens and the woods. She almost called out his name, but instead she followed him at a distance. She wanted to watch him for a moment longer, unobserved while her heart hammered with excitement and joy.

He stopped at a small bare patch of the woods, where a grouping of knee-high stones stood in a lop-sided circle. Celia hid behind a tree, watching him. He wore dark-gray trousers and a dark-blue button-up shirt, which he'd left untucked. It was a sign of how distracted he was. Normally Carter was dressed im-maculately, not a hair out of place, even when he was working on the grounds.

As Carter crouched by the old fairy circle, she admired the lean, muscular lines of his body. He held a small black velvet box.

"I bring a gift to the fairies. If magic still breathes within these woods, please accept my offer-ing." He smiled, as if remembering something won-derful from a long time ago. "This belonged to my mother, and I made a vow that it would only belong to the woman who owns my heart. She cannot take it, so I offer it to you. In exchange, I ask that you find a way to give her the life, the love, and the joy she deserves."

He straightened, his gaze still lingering on the circle of stones. Then he turned to leave. Celia waited just long enough for her to retrieve the box and open it unobserved. A sapphire ring wreathed in diamonds was nestled in the black velvet box. She recognized it at once. It was his mother's engagement ring. She'd seen it long ago as a child when she'd met Carter's mother. It was beautiful. She couldn't leave it here in the woods.

"Carter!" She called his name and rushed after him.

⚜

"CARTER!"

He heard his name echo through the woods. He

was going mad, imagining Celia calling to him when she was still in Scotland.

For a moment he thought the fairies in the glen were real, and that they were teasing him, calling him back to the circle where he'd left his mother's ring.

"Carter, wait!" Her voice was clearer now, all around him, echoing off the bark of the trees. It couldn't be his imagination, could it?

Carter turned, his heart pounding as he dared to believe the impossible. There, between the tall trees, a fairy queen stepped out to meet him in Celia's form.

"You can't leave this." She held out the small velvet box that contained his mother's ring. The one he'd left in the fairy circle.

Magic... The word brushed against his ears. Soft shadows pooled around them as the sun sank below the tops of the trees. There was indeed magic in this place, or perhaps it simply followed Celia wherever she went. There had been magic in Italy, magic in Scotland, and now here. With her.

"You're really here." It was all he could say as he took back the box, stunned.

An electric charge built between them as she stepped closer. "I am, and I'm not letting you go."

She reached up to cup his face and stood on her tiptoes to press her lips against his. The kiss seemed to burn him. The pain of the heart and pleasure of the body warred with each other as he put his hands on her hips. He shuddered as she pulled back.

"We can't..." He tried not to look at her. He knew why she was here, and he couldn't let her make that mistake.

She traced her fingers over his lips, and a tingle of desire shot down his spine. "We can."

"But..." He struggled to stay in control of himself. *What about Callum? What about Matthew? What about...?*

"Marry me, Carter Martin," Celia said.

"What?" Was this a dream? It had to be. His world started to spin, and he clung to her.

"I've been so foolish," she said. "Thinking that I can walk away from love, from you. I can't. I don't want to." She brushed her nose against his, teasing him with an almost kiss.

"What...what about Mathew?" he asked.

"We'll find a way to pay for his school and to pay Callum back. I'll live in Tristan's apartment in London to save money. I will come home on the weekends. I'll find a second job in town when I'm here." She curled her arms around his neck, pressing close to him, and he almost lost his mind. "I'll make it work. I swear."

"If we do this, you'll have to give up everything. I can't let you do that."

She sighed. "Don't you understand? You *are* everything. I can't believe that I've been denying the greatest truth my heart has been trying to tell me since the moment we met as children."

He couldn't speak. Despite everything she'd said, part of him still felt like he had to refuse her. There was no possible way she was thinking things through. She would regret this, given enough time. He was sure of it.

And yet, how could he say no? She'd offered him the secret wish of his heart.

"So...will you marry me? Uncle Edward gave us his blessing."

That, more than anything, shocked him out of the dreamlike state he'd fallen into ever since she'd emerged from the trees. "He did?"

"Yes. So...will you?" Celia asked again. He heard the note of fear in her voice. Fear because she thought he'd say no.

"Are you sure you want this?" he asked. Despite all her assurances, he had to ask.

She nodded. "More than anything."

His heart fluttered wildly. "Then yes. I will marry you."

Her face lit up, and suddenly they were kissing as if it were their lives depended on it. It was a kiss that set the world on fire. When they finally broke apart, it was growing dark.

Carter smiled. "When I was younger, I had such an amazing proposal planned, one that I knew I'd never get to make."

Celia smiled back. "Really? Well, you could get on one knee and ask me."

Carter chuckled. "It wouldn't be the same." He grinned down at her. "My original plan involved a flock of doves, fireworks..."

"Doves and fireworks?"

"And a suit of armor."

"Would you be riding in on a white horse too?"

"Naturally." He replied so seriously she started to laugh. "I might have even slayed a dragon or two for you."

"Then I definitely would have said yes." She clung to him as darkness descended in shades of purple around them.

They gazed at each other for a long moment and then he slowly lowered to one knee.

"Celia...I grew up alongside you, basking in light you cast. It was impossible not to love you. I don't deserve you, but," he cleared his throat. "The honor of being your husband would drive me every me to be worthy to you. Will you marry me?"

Celia cupped his face in her hands and kissed him again, her lips trembling as she whispered one word over and over between kisses. "Yes."

When he stood, he caught her by the waist and swung her around once, until they were both laughing.

"We should get back inside." He was reluctant to let go as she pressed herself against him. She held him tight for a moment, then stepped back and held out her left hand.

"I think I have earned my fairy sacrifice."

Laughing, he opened the velvet box and took out the sapphire ring. He slid it over her finger. It fit perfectly. His mother would have been thrilled.

He chuckled. "I suppose you are owed this after all the things Tristan and I got you to give up as a child."

She wrinkled her nose at the memory. "I'm still planning my revenge, you know."

"I think the ring makes us even, but feel free to avenge yourself upon Tristan." They both laughed, and he curled an arm around her waist as they walked back toward the house.

Tristan was there waiting for them, leaning against the open doorway.

"So...," he said. "You're going to be officially shagging my cousin?"

Celia's face reddened. "Tristan!"

"Officially. Forever." Carter held up Celia's hand with the ring, and Tristan's face split into a broad grin. He held out his hand to Carter.

"Welcome to the family."

Carter took it. They'd been best friends their entire lives. Now they would be family. It all seemed too good to be true.

"Carter." A deep voice came from behind. Tristan stepped aside to allow Edward Kingsley through.

"My lord," Carter said, a tad nervous despite having his blessing.

"I will be pleased to have you as my nephew-in-law."

"Thank you, my lord."

"Edward, please. Your family now, even if the formalities have not yet been observed." There was a soft gleam in his eyes that filled Carter with a strange feeling he couldn't quite explain. He had wanted approval from this man his entire life, but now, doing what he'd always feared would get him and his father cast out of their home, he'd seemed to win Lord Pembroke over. Life was a strange and wondrous thing.

"Now," Edward continued, "you'll want to file your paperwork in the register's office and post the banns in the church. I assume you will be married in our local parish?"

Carter and Celia shared a glance, then a smile. "Yes, we'd like that. Something small and private, of course." He wanted to reassure Lord Pembroke that he and Celia would stay within their means.

"Good. Why don't you both share the happy news with John? We can arrange the wedding after he and I returned from Wales."

Carter smiled as they headed upstairs to where his father was resting in one of the guest rooms. He was propped up in bed, a newspaper spread out across his lap.

"Carter!" John's face brightened. "And Miss Lynton? I thought you were in Scotland?"

Celia leaned into Carter's side.

"Father, Celia and I are to be married. Lord Pembroke has given us his blessing."

John stared at them, his eyes wide. "Married?"

"Yes. In a month, after you return from holiday."

"Carter, you're quite sure...?"

"We are," Celia said, understanding John's meaning. "We know it won't be easy, but we will face the challenges together."

John nodded to himself. "Well then, you have my blessing as well."

"Thank you, Father." Celia and Carter went over and hugged him.

"It will be nice to have a wedding. Tristan will no doubt be following in your steps in a few years. And think of the grandchildren." John smiled dreamily.

"Your mother would have loved to have been a grandmother."

"She would have," Carter agreed. He frowned, but only a little. There was not a day that went by that he did not miss her.

"Oh, off with you then. Let a man read in peace." John sniffed and made a show of ruffling his paper in his lap. Carter came over and hugged his father one more time. His father clasped his shoulder to keep him there a moment longer.

"She lives in you, you know? It's what made you such a good man. You have her heart. Raising you never made me miss her because I always see her in your eyes."

Celia hugged Carter's arm as he fought to keep his composure. He straightened his shoulders and nodded. "Get some rest, and recover your strength, Father. Those fish in Wales won't catch themselves."

He led Celia out of the room. They stood in the hall, gazing at each other for a long moment, filled with lingering disbelief.

"We're really doing this?" he asked.

"We are. But first I need to see Callum. Would you mind if I went to see him tonight? He's visiting a friend nearby."

Carter nodded. "Do you want me to go with you?"

She shook her head. "I should go alone. Wait up for me." She feathered a kiss on his lips, and then she was gone. But she would be back, and soon they would have the rest of their lives to share.

⁂

CELIA STOOD IN THE FOYER OF AN OLD MANSION. IT belonged to Bryson, the man Callum was in love with. She had been here once before, but only briefly, when she and Callum had made the arrangement she now intended to break. She stared at the old paintings and the sumptuous furnishings.

The butler returned after having gone to see if Callum was available. "Miss Lynton."

"Yes?"

"Mr. Radcliffe will see you in the parlor. This way please." The butler escorted her to a room at the end of the long hall. As she entered, she twisted the engagement ring on her finger anxiously, wondering if she should hide it until she was ready to tell him. Callum stood by the windows and turned at her entrance.

"Celia." He greeted her warmly, but she didn't miss the odd look in his eyes. "I suppose it's time we talked?"

"Actually..." She held her breath and raised her hand to show him her engagement ring. Callum's eyes fixed on the glinting sapphire. "Please don't be upset, Callum. I will find a way to pay you back for Matthew's tuition. I just couldn't go through with the marriage. I'm so sorry."

Callum was quiet a long moment and then slowly raised his own hand; a silver band encircled his ring finger. He smiled.

"It seems we both found we had to follow our hearts."

"You and Bryson are truly going to get married?"

"If you can believe it, yes."

"I can't, to be honest. You were certain your parents would disown you."

"It seems I'm a luckier man than I realized and I love someone who was determined to fight for me."

"You mean...?"

"Bryson reached out to my parents. Nothing dramatic, simply honest. The man has the soul of a poet, and I think that's what helped them understand. Yesterday, they called me from Inverness. I had no idea Bryson had already spoken to them."

"What happened?" Celia asked.

"My mother asked me if Bryson is the love of my life. I feared a confrontation, but in truth it was a confirmation she was looking for. She told me she loves me for who I am. To my surprise, my father said the same. A little reluctantly, perhaps, but he meant it. We'll have to discuss our options with a surrogate mother when the time comes for an heir, but I believe my parents are open to it."

"That's wonderful, Callum. I'm so happy for you." She hugged him, and he laughed.

"Thank you." He held up her hand, staring at the sapphire ring. "And you? Carter fought for you as well?"

Celia smiled. "I fought for him. He's too bound by duty to have ever asked me. But I convinced him. Eventually. He gave me his mother's ring."

"And your parents?"

"I haven't told them yet. That won't be easy, but my uncle fully supports us."

Callum gave her another squeeze. "Well, given how they rely on your uncle, I doubt they will cause much fuss."

"It won't matter to me if they do, but I don't want Matthew to feel the sting of their anger."

"We're doing the right thing," he said. "Even if it may be hard at times."

"Yes, but it will be worth it," she agreed. "And I promise, I will find a way to pay you back." It mattered to her that he knew she wouldn't take advantage of him, but Callum shook his head.

"Celia, you don't understand. My whole life I've convinced myself I had to live a certain way. I was ashamed and afraid to face my family, to face myself. But when you suggested we take a month to live our lives before this, it changed everything. I felt like a man who knew the date of his own execution and was determined to live every moment to the fullest before that. Long before it was over, I knew I couldn't live without Bryson. He found the courage to fight for us, even when I could not. I have you to thank for that. The way I see it, Matthew's tuition for the first semester is our wedding gift to you."

Celia's eyes blurred with tears, and she hugged Callum again. "I should get back to Carter. Invite me to your wedding, will you?"

"So long as you invite me to yours."

"I promise." Celia's heart was light in a way it had never been. All she had to deal with now was facing her parents and the nearly impossible task of finding a way to pay for the rest of Matthew's schooling. With the first semester paid for, she at least had time. She had Carter by her side, and that made her feel capable of anything. They would find a way.

When she returned to Pembroke, the house was quiet for the night. She hoped Carter was still waiting up for her. She reached his bedroom and eased the door open. He lay on his bed, lap covered in papers, and his computer lay on one of his thighs at an odd angle. His glasses were still on, but he was asleep, leaning back against the pillows. She checked her watch, smiling a little. It was after midnight, and he'd had a long and stressful day.

She carefully and quietly crawled onto the bed and eased the papers and computer off his lap and onto hers. She peeked at his work. Another proposal to a studio about using the estate as a filming location. She wanted so desperately for this to happen. But perhaps they'd have to settle for the miracle they'd already been given—each other.

She carefully laid his work on the nightstand and removed his glasses, setting them on top of the papers. She curled against him, breathing in the soft scent of cologne and something else that was just uniquely him.

She'd never told him this, but she'd gotten her revenge on him for the fairy queen stunt years ago. At least in part. She taken one of his sweaters and kept it for months, loving the fact that she could smell him in the warm, dark-colored wool.

Now she would have him for the rest of her life. She nuzzled his cheek before kissing him. He murmured something and wrapped his arms around her. She smiled and closed her eyes, dreaming of the wedding she never thought she'd have.

Sometimes there really was magic in the world.

❄ 14 ❄

Three weeks later

Garrick Kincade sat at his desk, poring over the estimates for the renovation Celia Lynton had provided. They'd arrived in a standard brown mailer, and along with it came a white card-sized envelope. He finally pushed aside the papers and opened the envelope.

A simple, elegant wedding invitation naming Celia Lynton and Carter Martin as the future bride and groom, along with the date and location of the event. No gifts requested, but charitable donations were allowed per the instructions. He chuckled over that as he'd put a call in to Ravenswood and placed a tuition donation toward Matthew Lynton's second semester just the other day.

Garrick reached for his cell phone, a smile on his lips. The invitation had reminded him of some unfinished business. He made calls to two people: Celia's boss, and a man he knew who ran a production company in Los Angeles. He was currently in England and would still be around at the time of the wedding.

Garrick booked a flight on his jet to London and then notified Mr. Dean of his intended departure. He sat back, glancing at the photo on his desk of Amelia. She had always loved romance stories. She had loved the very nature of love. When he'd said goodbye to her, he'd promised her that he would not give up on love.

But losing her had destroyed him. A man can't suffer heartbreak like that and remain unscathed. But even if he'd given up on himself, he could still help others like Celia and Carter. In his own way, he would be keeping his promise. He stroked a finger over the silver frame of her photo. In her memory, he would perform a few miracles.

For now, however, all he could do was help those who still had a chance at their own happily ever after.

⚜

CELIA ENTERED THE SMALL VINTAGE CLOTHING store she'd found in Soho. The gown she'd always dreamed she would wear to her wedding was far too expensive now, and she was determined to find something affordable. But affordable didn't have to preclude style or elegance.

"What are we looking for?" Kat asked her as she followed Celia down the rows of vintage wedding dresses hanging from the racks. Although she was American, she had fit right in with life in the English countryside and, more importantly, life with Tristan.

Celia had liked her from the beginning. They were kindred spirits, having both faced a difficult time trying to be with someone society insisted they could not be with.

As a future earl, Tristan's destiny wasn't with Kat, an American—at least according to Celia's uncle, once upon a time. And by a cruel twist of fate, Kat had been Tristan's stepsister when his mother married Kat's father, an American banker. Their love story had swept through London, first with the scandal of stepsiblings being romantically involved and then with Tristan's near death in a paparazzi-related car crash. But they had fought for their love, and in a way, it had shown Celia that she could fight for Carter.

Celia turned to Kat. She should have been stressed out given all that was happening, but surprisingly she wasn't. She simply felt free.

"I'm not sure what kind of dress I'm looking for. I'll know when I see it." Celia perused several more racks of wedding dresses before her hand froze on the last one. Her heart fluttered as she pulled it off the rack and nudged Kat.

"This might be it."

Kat eyed it, excited but uncertain. "Only one way to find out."

They ran to the changing rooms, where Celia stripped out of her clothes and pulled the dress on in a frenzy. She stepped out to get Kat's reaction.

"Oh. My. God." Kat paused between each word, her eyes wide. "Celia...you look *amazing*."

Celia turned to find the nearest mirror. Her breath caught, and her eyes stung with tears. Kat was right. It was perfect. Absolutely perfect. And it wouldn't cost a fortune.

"What about this?" Kat held up a small white Juliet cap with a veil that would cover her face. It was perfect, just like the dress. The only thing left on her list was to talk to her parents. She had sent out secret invitations last week to a handful of people she trusted. But soon her parents would figure things out, and she would have to face them.

Celia changed back into her clothes and paid for her dress and veil. Once back at Pembroke, Kat returned to the main house with their shopping bags while Celia began the long walk to the small cottage at the back of the estate.

Her mother and father, were in the small parlor that now operated as her father's office. He was sifting through account statements, frowning, while her mother read a fashion magazine. Celia couldn't help but sigh. This was the life her mother expected for her. High fashion, parties, trips across the world, and engaging with "important" people.

But I don't want that. I want Carter.

"Mother, Father? I need to speak with you."

Her parents both looked at her. "Ah, Celia," her father began. "I've been thinking—isn't it about time we announced your engagement to Callum?"

"Actually, no... He's getting married to someone else."

"What?" her father cried out in shock.

"In a week."

"What?" her mother yelled.

"To a very charming man. Turns out I wasn't his type at all."

"*What?*" they screeched together.

She had to admit, as much as she'd dreaded this conversation, that part had been fun. Her parents had never suspected Callum was gay.

Her mother dropped the fashion magazine and stared at her in horror. "But... How? You've known Callum for years. You said everything had been arranged."

Celia drew in a breath. "Yes, I've known Callum for years. But we both knew there was no love in this match, only a convenient way to avoid inconvenience. We were trying to hide from our problems, but neither of us was going to be happy." She studied their faces. Her mother was shocked, her father skeptical.

"If this is about that Martin boy...," Hensley began.

"He's not a boy, Father. He happens to be my fiancé. We're to be married in two days. You are both invited, provided that you agree to behave. I would like you to walk me down the aisle, Father."

Her mother's eyes threatened to roll back in her head, like she was going to faint and fall over backward.

"But what about Matthew?" her father sputtered. "Callum was going to pay for Ravenswood. You cannot think only of yourself. What about your family?" Her father was quick to point out her duty, just as she'd expected him to.

"Celia?" Her brother's voice made them all suddenly stop. Matthew stood only a few feet behind her, eyes wide. Nobody had seen him enter.

"Matthew." She wanted to embrace him, but he'd never been one for hugging, so she kept her distance.

"You were going to marry someone for me? So I could go to that school?" Matthew's look of hurt stung Celia's heart.

"Yes, I was."

"But you're not anymore?"

"I'm sorry, Matthew. We weren't in love." Celia played with the ring on her finger. "I asked Carter to marry me."

"Celia, you can't marry that boy," her mother said. "You have to take care of Matthew."

"No, she doesn't." Matthew stepped in front of Celia. "If I can't afford to go to Ravenswood, then I won't go. Celia can't marry someone she doesn't love. Not for me."

Celia had never seen her brother so focused, so engaged in the affairs of others before. And he was defending her.

"Matthew," their father protested. "Now see here—"

"No," Matthew snapped. "She's always taken care of me. She's given up more for me than you ever have. I won't allow her to give up this." He turned to look at her. "When is the wedding?"

"In two days, at the old Pembroke parish church."

"I'll be there," Matthew promised. "If Father doesn't come, I will walk you down the aisle."

"Thank you." She shot her parents one last look. She could tell by the looks on their faces that it would do no good to stay any longer. Either they would come around or they wouldn't, but she was done living up to their expectations.

She and Carter had their whole lives to look forward to, and she was not about to let them ruin another minute of it. With one more smile at Matthew, she turned and walked away.

❦

Tristan stood beside Carter in front of the small altar in the cozy little cobblestone church just two miles from the Pembroke estate. Carter fought the urge to adjust his pale-blue silk tie and failed.

Tristan smirked. "You've checked it four times already. It's fine. But what about you? Are you prepared for this?"

"I've been prepared since the moment I met her."

"You were two years old," Tristan reminded him.

"And I knew it then."

He looked over the first couple of pews. Callum Radcliffe and his fiancé, Bryson, were in the second row. Lord Pembroke, Carter's father, Aunt Holly and Celia's brother were in the first row. Garrick Kincade had flown in from Scotland. When Garrick noticed Carter looking at him, he winked. Carter returned the wink with a small nod.

The music started as the organist one in the balcony began to play "Canon in D" by Pachelbel. The doors of the church opened and Kat entered, wearing a pale-rose knee-length gown. She held a small bouquet of lilies and walked in even paces toward the altar.

"You're next, you know," Carter warned Tristan with a grin.

"I know," Tristan said, his gaze full of adoration as Kat joined them at the altar and took her place.

Then the doors opened again and Celia stood

there, a larger bouquet of lilies in her hands. Beside her stood her father. Carter couldn't believe it. Her father had come?

Celia came forward, her pale ivory gown whispering on the burgundy carpet leading up to the altar. Her gown was stunning. A long-sleeved lace bodice and a pleated silk faille skirt and a silk faille cummerbund and train made Celia look like the fairy queen he had always teased her about being.

A small Juliet-style cap held her short veil in place. The veil allowed her face to be visible as she passed through the muted beams of sunlight that shown through the stained-glass windows. It was an unforgettable moment, seeing the woman he loved bathed in splashes of brilliant color. For a second, Carter forgot to breathe. Her beauty had cast a spell over him. There was no doubt in his mind that he was about to become the luckiest man on earth.

As Celia reached the altar, her father stepped forward to transfer her to him. He spoke softly to Carter, so only he could hear.

"Make her happy."

Carter nodded. "I will."

Mr. Lynton stepped back and took his place beside Lord Pembroke in the first row. The church doors opened again, and Celia's mother slipped in. She was frowning, but she took a seat at the back. It would take longer to win Bernadette over, it seemed, but they would find a way.

Celia's gaze met his as she joined him before the clergyman.

"Last chance to change your mind," she whispered, then bit her bottom lip. He wanted to lift the veil and kiss her right then and there.

"There is nothing in the world that I want more than you."

He took her hands in his, never once looking away as the ceremony began. He was lost in her eyes, the sunlight of her smile, and the soft laugh that escaped her lips when she had to nudge him to complete his vows because he was distracted by her. He wanted to remember every detail of this day, from the way the pearl buttons of her gown shimmered like frozen raindrops to the way her skin flushed beneath the lace just above her breasts.

When the clergyman pronounced them man and wife, he could only smile. There were no words to describe the swell of joy rushing through him, filling every cell of his body until he felt his blood hum in his veins.

Tristan slapped him on the back. "Welcome to the family, Carter."

"Th-thank you," he replied, somewhat shocked by how happy he was. He had grown so used to the suffering that came with knowing one's place and yet seeing his heart's desire beyond it. Yet here he was, celebrating his marriage to the woman of his dreams. He wavered a little and lost his footing.

Tristan caught him by one shoulder. "Whoa, steady on," Tristan murmured. "No fainting on your wedding day."

The married couple were soon surrounded by their closest friends and family, everyone congratulating them. Even Celia's parents approached. Carter shook her father's hand and nodded politely to her mother.

"You'll be as poor as church mice, but at least the grandchildren will be beautiful," Bernadette said, still somewhat haughty.

"Where will you two live?" Hensley said, cutting in. "Celia is in London, and you're here."

"They'll be living here part of the year," Edward announced. "One of the old hunting lodges is habitable with a bit of repairs, and the cost won't be much. The estate can afford to tidy it up for you."

"But...," Celia began, no doubt worried about her

position at the architectural firm if she couldn't work in London year-round.

"I've already spoken to your employer. He was quite happy to have his IT department set you up for remote office space. You should only have to go to London once or twice a week. In exchange, I will be hosting your firm's Christmas parties each year here at the house. And..." Edward glanced toward Matthew. "I did try to make a payment on Matthew's tuition, but it seems someone has taken care of the first year already. They said it was a charitable donation in honor of your wedding. Given this unforeseen boon, I may be able to pay for his second year of schooling."

Bernadette's jaw dropped and then she genuinely smiled at her older brother. "Oh, Edward..."

"Bernie, I expect you and Hensley to step up while you live at the estate. There's plenty of work now that John is retiring. And I'd rather like to step down myself in many areas, particularly those which require public appearances. I believe you two would be well suited to being the public face of the family on those occasions where I wish to remain at home."

Hensley cleared his throat and nodded solemnly. "Yes, I think that's a good idea. Let me know what to do, and I'll see it done."

"And..." Garrick now stepped forward, holding out a business card. "I believe, if you contact this production company, you'll find the interest in your estate you've been hoping for." Carter accepted the card and stared at the name of the company and the owner's contact info. It was a successful studio that put together many period dramas. There was just one problem.

"I'm afraid I've already contacted them, and they said they were looking into other locations," said Carter.

Garrick grinned. "You'll find them more receptive

this time around," he said. "Sometimes it's persistence that matters most in the entertainment business."

Carter had to fight to keep his hand from shaking as he pocketed the business card. "Thank you, Lord Kincade, truly."

He looked at his bride and saw her bottom lip quivering. He curled an arm around her waist and pulled her against him. She wrapped her arms around his neck, her entire body now shaking.

"Celia," he breathed in her ear. "Please, love, you know I can't bear to see you cry."

"It's just...we never thought..."

"But it happened. Miracles do happen, love." He kissed her cheek and then realized that more of the other guests were watching them with concern. Kat came over and patted Celia's back.

"Everything okay?" she asked.

"She's just a bit overwhelmed by everything."

Kat grinned. "Who wouldn't be? It's like the stars finally aligned for you two."

"Better than them being crossed, I would think," Tristan added with a laugh.

"It certainly is," Carter agreed. He bent his head toward Celia and kissed her. He couldn't remember a time when he hadn't loved her, and now she was finally his. All around them he could feel the pulse of magic, intangible yet present, gently coloring the world around them.

She is forever mine, and I shall always be forever hers.

EPILOGUE

Garrick Kincade bid farewell to the happily married couple and climbed into the Porsche roadster he'd rented. As he drove down the country roads, he smiled a little at the thought that he'd been able to help them out as much as he had. Amelia would have approved.

He wasn't sure how long he'd been driving before he noticed a car pulled over on the side of the road. Two people stood on either side of the vehicle, shouting at each other. One of them, a pretty brunette, struggled to get her suitcase out of the back seat. The man waved one arm around, clearly angry.

Garrick pulled his car up behind theirs and got out, picking up only the last bit of their conversation.

"No more excuses. I've had it, Stephen!" The woman's voice trembled even as she shouted at him.

"Ava, come on—she didn't mean anything to me."

"Oh yeah?" Ava shouted. "When you were on top of her in bed, she didn't mean anything? You just fell naked on top of a waitress?"

"I told you, I was drunk!"

"And I'd have to be twice as drunk to buy *that* excuse." Ava managed to free her suitcase from the car and nearly tumbled backward with the unexpected weight of it.

"Pardon me," Garrick began, but the couple continued to argue.

"So you're going to walk all the way back to London?" Stephen's face had turned an unpleasant shade of red.

"It's better than riding back with you, you cheating bastard!" Ava started to roll her suitcase away from the car.

"Excuse me, miss, are you all right?" Garrick called out. Stephen and Ava both finally noticed him.

"She's fine," Stephen said.

"I'm anything but." Ava glanced at Stephen and then looked to Garrick. "Are you headed to London?"

"As it so happens, yes. Would you like a ride?"

Ava looked him over and then nodded. "Thanks. I'd appreciate it." She started walking toward Garrick's car.

"Ava, you're not getting in some stranger's car, are you? Don't be crazy. What if he's a serial killer?"

Ava looked Garrick up and down. "Are you?" she asked him flatly.

"Er... No. I most certainly am not. I'm Scottish, actually." He wasn't sure why he added that, other than the fact that these two were clearly American.

"Good enough for me." Ava dragged her bag to his car and waited for him to unlock it. He popped the boot and placed her suitcase inside. Stephen came over, but Garrick carefully stepped between them.

"Get out of my way," Stephen growled.

"I'm afraid I can't do that. The lady doesn't want to be with you right now. If she wishes to contact you later, I'm sure she will."

"Fat chance of that. Can we leave now, please?" Ava asked Garrick.

"Er... Yes." He escorted her to the passenger side of his car and let her inside. Then he faced Stephen down one more time.

"You can't just leave with my girlfriend."

"*Ex*-girlfriend," Ava shouted from the car.

"As she says...," Garrick said.

"Ava, come on!" Stephen shouted over Garrick's shoulder, but Ava shook her head.

"We're done. I'll find my own way home." She looked at Garrick. "Can we please just leave?"

"Yes, of course." Garrick got into the car and started the engine. Ava stared straight ahead as they drove around Stephen's car and headed down the road.

"Are you really all right, miss?"

"It's Ava, Ava Chase. I was going to walk back to London because my boyfriend was cheating on me. Of course I'm not all right."

"Yes, well...I'm sorry about that." Garrick felt strange having a woman in his car, especially an attractive one with such a fiery spirit. He hadn't missed the way the light brought out the different shades of brown in her hair and the way her face was perfectly proportioned, from her full lips to her almond-shaped hazel eyes. They were the rare sort of honey color that one didn't often see.

"I'm Garrick Kincade." He held out his left hand to her, and she shook it, blushing a little.

"I'm crazy, aren't I? For getting in a car with a stranger?" She seemed to be partly talking to herself.

"I think some would consider walking to London crazier," he said.

"You know what I mean."

Garrick smiled. "I suppose it wasn't the wisest thing to do, but I assure you I am a gentleman, and that does mean rescuing someone in distress. I'm happy to take you anywhere you'd like to go."

"Anywhere?" She smiled sadly. "I'm tempted to ask you to take me to Scotland. It's where Stephen and I..." She faltered. "Where we were supposed to go next."

"Well, I am scheduled for a flight back there in three hours. There's room on the plane..."

"What do you mean? You have another ticket?"

"You might say I have all the tickets." Garrick chuckled. "I have a private jet, just a small one. I only need to add your name to the passenger list if you wish to come. I'd be quite happy to have you join me."

"Oh...I couldn't," Ava protested. But Garrick saw a hint of desperation in her eyes.

"Please, allow me to show you that chivalry isn't dead. At least on this side of the pond."

Ava bit her lip, but he could see the corners of her mouth twitch with a little smile.

"Okay... Okay. Yes. Let's do it. If Stephen can sleep with a waitress, I can accept a free ride to Scotland, right? All's fair in love and war." Their eyes met, and for the first time in over a year he felt something. Not just something but a pang of desire—fleeting, fading, but real nonetheless.

It was as though his heart had been given an electric shock and was beating again after years of deathly silence. This American's plight had somehow brought him back to life.

Wherever his Amelia was now, she was probably giggling. She had wanted him to live again, not hide himself away in a shell of heartbreak.

He smiled at Ava, then focused back on the road. Was he ready to move on? He didn't want to be, but perhaps he was.

Regardless, it couldn't hurt to spend a little more time with Ava Chase.

THANK YOU SO MUCH FOR READING *FOREVER BE MINE*!

If you love this story and want to read more about Garrick and Ava in the next book, please

leave a review for it and tell your friends! Showing a book love, helps the authors write the next book in the series!

The best way to know when a new book is released in this series is to do one or all of the following:

For Lauren Smith:

Join Lauren Smith's Newsletter: http:// laurensmithbooks.com/free-books-and- newsletter/

Follow Lauren on BookBub: https://www. bookbub.com/authors/lauren-smith

Join Lauren Smith's Facebook VIP Reader Group called Lauren Smith's League: https:// www.facebook.com/groups/400377546765661/

Now, in case you haven't read Tristan and Kat's story, you don't want to miss this three chapter preview of *Forbidden*! Turn the page now to start reading this stream romance about another British bad boy!

FORBIDDEN
love in london series
USA TODAY BEST SELLING AUTHOR
lauren smith

FORBIDDEN

CHAPTER 1

"Tonight is the start of my grand adventure. And since it's my birthday, you guys are welcome to join in the fun." Kat Roberts grinned as she spread out the folded piece of paper on the table so her friends Lacy and Mark could see.

They were nestled in the corner of the Pickerel Inn just outside Magdalene College in Cambridge, catching a brief break from studying for exams. The pub was full of other students, all enjoying the relaxed atmosphere and the fish and chips the pub served late into the night.

"What on earth is that?" Lacy asked as she brushed her hair back from her face and peered at the list.

Kat tapped the paper. "A list of ten things every undergraduate should do while studying and living in Cambridge. Number one? Drink a glass of Nelson's Revenge at the Pickerel Inn pub on Magdalene Street."

Mark, Lacy's boyfriend, chuckled. "Have too many Nelsons and he'll definitely get his revenge. You Americans aren't used to our stout ales."

Kat was only half-listening as she studied the list, contemplating the other suggestions it gave. She'd moved to England in August to start college while her dad worked in London, and now more than ever she wanted to do something wild, something fun and crazy. Her parents had divorced when she was a kid, and she'd been living with her father, whose job entailed frequent corporate moves. She'd been too afraid to get close to people and break out of her shell. She didn't want to make connections with people only to have to leave and never see them again. It reminded her too much of when her mother had left.

But that's all changed. I'm finally living in one place for three years. I'm making friends here. Roots. For the first time I can really live.

Now she yearned for an adventure. She wasn't used to being wild and crazy or doing things out of her comfort zone, but she wanted to be that way.

Baby steps, she had to remind herself. That's why she'd picked this list from an online article about attending school in Cambridge. It had fun things for her to do. Things she might not have otherwise tried. Now that she'd settled into her classes and schoolwork, she could focus on enjoying the whole college experience. She'd picked an easy item from the list first—drinking a pint here at the Pickerel—but she'd work her way up to the bigger items soon.

Mark leaned forward, his elbows propped on the old wooden table. "Is this really all we get to do to help you celebrate your nineteenth birthday?"

"He's right, Kat. We should be doing something really fun tonight. Like going clubbing!" Lacy curved her lips in a charming but teasing smile that under other circumstances would've made Kat laugh.

"Clubbing? Lacy, you know I can't dance. I'd fall flat on my face. Maybe if I drink enough you can talk me into it." Kat winked at her friend and gulped down more of the cider and beer blend she had ordered. It wasn't strong, but she wanted to get warmed up before going for the Nelson's Revenge.

Lacy grinned. "You're officially nineteen, and as this is your first semester at college, we need to make something amazing happen. Leave high school behind. This is your chance. Let's go dancing, meet some hot guys." She jerked her head suggestively toward a nearby table where a group of decent-looking men were watching them, pints in hand and friendly smiles on their faces. She nudged Mark in the ribs. "Right?" She winked.

Mark put an arm around Lacy's shoulders and shook his head, silently laughing. "You have a hot guy right here for you, no need to find a new one," he teased.

Lacy rolled her eyes. "You know what I mean, *for Kat*. She needs some action."

Kat couldn't disagree. She'd never really dated in high school since she and her dad had moved every couple of years. Maybe Lacy was right. Now was the time to give it a try.

"First I'll drink my pint, then I'll work my way up to meeting hot guys. How's that?"

Mark shook his head. "I think you're underestimating your appeal. British blokes like me would love to date an American. You'll have no trouble getting a guy." He nodded at the same group of men his girlfriend had pointed out. "Start with them. They look nice enough, and if they aren't, I'll beat them up for you." Mark put up his fists with a silly, goonish expression that made Kat and Lacy giggle.

Kat adored her new friends. She'd only known them since August, but something about them, their natural warmth, the way they opened up to her, made her feel like she'd known them for years.

Maybe it was the magic of the city, too. Ever since she'd come here for university, this little Elizabethan-era town had captivated her. Between the shops tucked in crooked, wandering alleys and the tolling bells of the various colleges throughout the day, Kat had been bewitched by this tiny part of the world. It was more of a home for her than any other place she'd ever lived.

"Well, don't tell me you're afraid to give it a go?" Mark laughed.

His brown eyes were dark and full of brotherly mischief, offering a friendship Kat hadn't thought she'd find again since she'd left her last high school boyfriend behind. She and Ben had been good friends, more than she'd ever thought possible with a guy. Like him, Mark was easygoing, with a ready smile and a playful attitude that put her at ease.

She and Ben hadn't been serious, and calling him a boyfriend was really more of a stretch. They'd hung out but never even kissed. When she'd confessed this to Lacy, her friend had gasped and immediately informed her that what she and Ben hadn't been a "real" relationship.

Kat jerked herself out of the spiral her thoughts had taken and focused on her friends. She tipped back her drink and finished it. She couldn't believe it was close to the end of November, and the term was winding down. As much as she'd enjoyed her classes, she was glad for the upcoming winter break. What better way to start the holidays than getting a jumpstart on her "Operation Adventure."

When the front door of the pub suddenly opened, an icy wind cut through the cozy atmosphere of the building. Despite the dim gold light cast by the fixtures in the pub, Kat could see more than one person at the surrounding tables muttering, clutching at their coats and glancing toward the front door.

"Oh my," Lacy murmured, her brown eyes all soft and dreamy as she stared at something behind Kat.

Mark coughed, catching Lacy's attention, but Kat was already turning around in her seat. For some reason all of the breath left her body and she blinked, completely spellbound.

There, framed in the doorway, was a living, breathing god. When he closed the door behind him, snowflakes swirled and eddied around him, clinging to his dark hair and his black knee-length pea coat. He made her think of Hades, the dark god of the Netherworld, in search of his sweet, innocent lover Persephone.

Kat would never have thought she'd describe a man in such terms, but this man…oh yes, the description was perfect. So perfect it almost hurt to look at him. The kind of gorgeous that made a woman's body respond instantly. A slow wave of heat overtook Kat as she stared at him, and she clamped her thighs together when a slow throb began to build in her lower abdomen.

Now that's the sort of man I want to get involved with. One who would sweep me away, make me forget who I used to be, and show me who I might become. A woman who lives life on the edge, who explores dark passions and truly experiences life. The thought of being with a man like him… it felt right to want him.

The decent-looking guys a few tables away had nothing on this man. And that was just it: He was a man. Nothing about him screamed "college student." The way he walked, in an almost predatory, graceful movement, sucked her in, and she couldn't look away. He was the sort of man who would stop every woman in her tracks as he strode past, demanding their attention, *their desire…*

His eyes swept over the room, not even noticing her.

No surprise. She was just another undergraduate student bundled up in jeans, a thick sweater, and boots.

Not like him.

A pinch of pain in her chest made her set her cider down and blink rapidly. She'd never minded being invisible before, but looking at this sexy god of a man...she wanted to get his attention. It was a stupid, girlish feeling, but she wanted him to look her way, see her. The pull he had on her was strange, magnetic, like nothing she'd ever felt before. It was as though something inside her was pulling her toward him, erasing everything else around him.

Look my way, she silently begged.

But he didn't. A knot of disappointment tightened in her chest. There was no way he'd ever notice her.

He's way out of my league. We're in different galaxies.

Even knowing this, she couldn't stop looking at him. This man looked expensive, from his shiny, black boots to the sleek look of his trousers and coat. When her gaze locked on his face, she was lost in a study of him. His aristocratic features were stunning. The man had a jawline that looked like it had been cut from marble, and a straight patrician nose that created an aura of entitled ease. He knew he was attractive and exactly how his mere presence could affect a room.

The hint of an arrogant smile played upon his full, sensual lips, so faint that she wondered if she was imagining it. And there was something about how he surveyed the room, like a ruler among his subjects. It wasn't surprising. Like King Arthur, but with dark, chocolate hair rather than fair. He was tall and lean with wide shoulders, and she could tell there were muscles beneath those fine clothes by the way the fabric clung to him. As he strode over to the bar and leaned against it to order a drink, the focus of the room went with him.

A stir of whispers started up a table behind Kat, Lacy, and Mark. A group of college students, three girls, were watching the new stranger, too. Their heads were bent together, and their hushed voices carried just enough that Kat caught snippets of their conversation.

"I think that's....yes, I'm sure it's him. You go, Talia, ask him..." one girl suggested.

"No way, if that's who he is...He'd never...Too hot though right? I'd let him do anything to me..." More giggles. "Can you imagine having sex with him? I heard he's a god in bed. I'd like Mr. Sexy to take me home."

The third girl fanned herself. "He's got a bad reputation, though...total heartbreaker. Never dates, only fucks them, you know...but I'll be damned if I don't want to..."

The conversation was muffled when a waiter delivered the girls more beers, and Kat couldn't hear anything else. So whoever Mr. Sexy was...these girls knew him or knew *of him*. And he had a bad reputation? What kind of bad reputation?

Kat turned her focus back to him, gazing longingly, watching him slide his black leather gloves off to reveal long fingers and elegant but masculine hands. A gold signet ring gleamed on the little finger of his left hand. She swallowed hard as a wave of heat rippled through her so fast beads of sweat gathered at her temples. She reached for her empty glass of cider again, never taking her eyes off the gorgeous man.

"You should probably go get your pint of Nelson's Revenge," Lacy said. "I really want to go clubbing, so get that drink, check it off your list, and let's go!"

Her friend's voice seemed to break through the odd sort of fog in her head. She didn't want to leave this little pub and go dancing, not when a man like *him* was here. She could have watched him all night.

Clubbing was definitely not on the list of things she'd like to do, but it would get her out of her shell. Of course, it would really help if she had that drink. And getting that drink meant a chance to get close to the beautiful stranger.

"Okay, be back in a second." She pushed her chair and headed toward the bar. The crowd was thick around the bartender, and Kat could barely see him over the heads of the students laughing and talking as they leaned against the antique wood bar. The only empty spot against the counter was next to Mr. Sexy...

Raising her chin, she started to walk in his direction, attempting to play it cool, like she wasn't going to get turned on just by standing so close to this god of a man.

He probably won't even look at me...but what if he does? Gotta be cool....I can handle this, right?

A second before she reached him, her right foot slipped in a spot of melted snow.

"Ahh!" Kat gasped as she tried to catch herself, but she careened straight into the beautiful stranger. Normally she wouldn't have been so clumsy, but she'd been too focused on him and hadn't been watching the floor. Plenty of people had been slipping all night.

"Oomph," he grunted and threw his arms out, pulling her to his chest.

Kat's head fell back as she clung to his shoulders. He was tall, deliciously so, and her head only just reached the bottom of his chin. His hair was swept back from his face, but it fell across his eyes as he stared down at her, and the light kissed the dark brown strands with a faint hint of gold. The color of his eyes was...stunning and made her almost dizzy when she stared. Like losing herself in a kaleidoscope of blue and green in endless splintering shafts.

Her knees wobbled, and she dug her hands harder into his shoulders, trying to stay on her feet.

What is wrong with me?

"Hello, darling, are you all right? Bit of a slick spot, eh?"

That rich voice, such decadent, sinful syllables uttered in that oh-so-perfect English accent, made Kat quiver inside. What was it about accents? They made a girl think strange, silly things, like asking him to talk dirty to her. Oh, the things he could say that would melt her into a puddle just like the snow at his feet. It might kill her with pleasure. The thought was so unlike her that she blinked. There was something about this man that made her want things she'd been hesitant to want before now. Like hot, sweaty sex. She was still a virgin, and yet this man was making her want to strip down naked and jump into the nearest bed with him.

"I..."

His hands were still holding her waist, his body pressed against hers. She couldn't think; her brain short-circuited. His hands on her, so hot to the touch...They were standing so close, faces mere inches apart, and the world around her seemed to burn with a heat along her skin. Her breath quickened.

Kat struggled to think logically, but all she could think about was how much she wanted to kiss him.

"Are you able to stand on your own?" He smiled, the single flirty twist of his lips making her knees buckle again.

What the heck? She'd never had a problem with her legs working before.

"Er...yes," she finally managed to say.

"Good." His hands dropped, but the movement felt reluctant. He trailed his hands down her body, the light but suggestive skimming of his palms over her waist, then her hips, sent little throbbing pulses throughout her entire body. He didn't step away, either, but kept close to her, his eyes still fixed on her face. "I'm glad to have prevented a nasty fall."

Before she could reply, the bartender leaned over the counter and spoke. "What can I get you?"

Mr. Tall and Sexy shifted slightly, allowing Kat to slip into the space next to him, their shoulders and arms touching as she answered.

"I'll have a pint of Nelson's Revenge, please."

The stranger next to her chuckled. "Are you sure about that?" he asked. "That's a stiff drink and likely to bring tears to your eyes." There was a hint of teasing in his tone, and Kat couldn't resist responding.

"I'm sure. Besides, I'm more likely to start crying at the sight of a butterfly than a stout ale." She laughed, then realized what'd she said and blushed.

The man angled his body toward her, propping one arm on the counter as he stared down at her.

"Butterflies make you cry? What on earth for? Don't tell me you're afraid of them." Humor heated those blue-green eyes of his, and she felt an answering heat sweep through her body.

"I...well, it's silly really..." She hedged. She didn't normally open up to people, let alone strange, beautiful men in pubs. But there was something about the way he was watching her, his intense focus on her and his interest in what she was saying, that gave her courage to continue.

"I used to live in Texas with my dad, and we saw monarch butterflies when they migrated. But now with their habitats dying out, I rarely see them. When I do get lucky and one flies past me, it's beautiful...and sad." She shrugged her shoulders, glancing away. "I know that sounds silly."

"Not at all," he murmured softly. "No sillier than how I feel when I look at stained glass windows. It's the same for me, that mixture of melancholy and beauty. It's not often I meet someone else who thinks about things like that." His intense scrutiny tore her in two directions, between the need to squirm and to go very still.

The man possessed an overpowering, seductive and masculine presence. She caught the scent of pine and something clean and crisp that sparked her other senses to life. It encompassed her like some dark spell, leaving her with a desperate need to stay close to him. The things those girls had whispered about him came rushing back..."*bad reputation*"..."*god in bed*"...Whoever he was didn't matter, she just *wanted* him. Wanted to curl her arms around his neck and get as close to him as possible.

"I think about that stuff all the time," she said, unable to tear her gaze away from his.

He lifted his glass to his lips and sipped. It wasn't ale he was drinking but something else, a dark, warm gold color, probably Scotch. She realized she must have been staring at his mouth when he licked his lips and spoke again.

"Keep staring at me like that and I'm liable to kiss you."

CHAPTER 2

Desire and hunger lit up his eyes, heating the strange mixture of blue and green. It almost made her forget that she was talking to a stranger. It *really* was possible to lose yourself in someone's eyes. Maybe the poets weren't wrong about love at first sight. She didn't love this man, but she was...captivated by him, which felt like love, in a strange sort of way. The lightness of her head, the wobbly knees, the fascination with him.

"There's nothing stopping you from kissing me," she breathed. Her heart was pounding against her ribs as excitement skittered through her. Would he accept the challenge and kiss her?

His eyes softened, but there was a dangerous glint to his expression, one that warned her that if he kissed her...it wouldn't be chaste, wouldn't be sweet. It would be the sort of kiss that made a girl forget where she was and moan helplessly for more.

They were mere inches apart now...When had she leaned into him? Somehow she had shifted closer, fixated on his mouth, the full sensual lips. The bit of the cider ale she'd been drinking earlier made her thoughts a bit muddy. Well, all but one thought.

I want him to kiss me. If he won't, I'll kiss him first.

Before she let herself think better of it, she seized

the chance to be reckless and rocked up on her tiptoes, curling her fingers into the lapels of his coat as she kissed him. *Hard*. It was wild, the way she let go and just gave herself into kissing him. Her own sexy stranger...

His hands gripped her waist, fingers digging in slightly, making tingles of excitement shoot down her spine, clear to her toes. His lips were soft and warm, moving against hers hungrily. When he angled his face, he caressed her lips with his tongue. The startling, erotic feel of it had her mouth parting, and he thrust inside. The little teasing strokes of his tongue against hers created shivers deep in her belly. He overwhelmed all of her senses, and Kat couldn't catch her breath. There was no escaping his strong hold, and she didn't want to. His lips were a drug, and she couldn't get enough.

Every cell in her body pulsed and hummed to life when the kiss turned slightly rough, as he nipped her bottom lip. She rocked her body into his, desperate to get closer, to feel him completely surrounding her.

All mine. She smiled against his lips just as their bodies separated a few inches and she gasped for a breath. Blood pounded against her temples, and she panted and glanced up at him. Stark, raw lust burned like coals behind his eyes as he stared down at her, an almost animal ferocity in his expression.

"That was—"

Before she could finish, he curled an arm around her waist and pulled her flush against him for another kiss. The touch of his lips this time was feather light...as though he were savoring her. A simple, almost innocent brush of mouths, before she shivered, and a little moan of longing escaped. Suddenly he rotated her, pinning her against the bar, his mouth taking her hungrily, seeking entrance to hers. She parted her lips, more from surprise than anything else. When his tongue slid in and teased hers, she whimpered. The bare hint of stubble rasped against her skin as he kissed her, making her sensitive to every sensation.

More, I need more of this...

No one she'd dated in high school had kissed like this, as though he had all night to taste her, explore her, excite her. Nothing else mattered, nothing but this man and his life-altering, seductive lips.

When his mouth parted from hers, she blinked and stared up at him, wondrously dazed.

"You were too tempting to resist. Makes a man hungry for more when a woman looks at him like that." He brushed the pad of his thumb over her swollen lips, his eyes tracing the shape, along with his finger.

"Like what?" she asked, fascinated by his words just as much as his hands and the way they touched her.

His laugh was dark and rich like a pint of Guinness. "Like she needs to be kissed, to be *taken* by a man who knows just what to do to make her moan with pleasure."

Taken...the word was heavy, dark, forbidding and yet it filled her with a secret thrill. She could picture this man taking her, doing a thousand erotic things that would blow her mind and her body apart.

She struggled to respond, but what could she say to the man who'd just changed her life with one mind-blowing kiss and talked to her about how he could make a woman moan with pleasure? Had she really just made out with a complete and total stranger? She needed to do something, *anything*, to lessen the suddenly awkward moment.

She thrust out her hand and said, "I'm Katherine Roberts, but everyone calls me Kat." It felt silly to introduce herself after the kiss they'd shared, but she did it anyway.

The man stared at her hand and then took it,

raising it to his lips rather than shaking it. He brushed his mouth over the backs of her knuckles in a caress, like an old world prince greeting a lady. Her heart fluttered inside her chest at the little romantic act. She'd never met a man who'd done that before, and it made her imagine what it might feel like to have his lips on other parts of her body.

"Tristan Kingsley. It's been quite the pleasure meeting you." The blue-green of his eyes rippled with glints of light like a summer lake at noon. "I'd like to kiss you again—"

"Tristan! There you are!" A light, feminine voice shook Kat out of her hazy daydreams of being wrapped in his arms again.

A tall blonde with stunning, classical features and a killer sense of style stood in the pub's doorway, watching Tristan and Kat. Her pink lips were curved up in an excited smile, and her blue eyes were bright and merry.

"So sorry I'm late. The snow is quite wretched on the roads," she said as she strode over in her too perfect high-heeled boots and skinny jeans.

Kat wanted to melt into the floor but shuffled her own scuffed boots instead. Her face heated when Tristan released her hand and glanced at the blonde woman. Just like that, Kat was forgotten as he stepped around her. So much for her dreams of a man like that paying attention to her. She was just another passing fancy while he waited for his girlfriend to show up. A wave of nausea mixed with anxiety rolled through her stomach. This was why she was afraid to take risks. Because rejection hurt like hell.

"Celia!" Tristan grinned, as he opened his arms to embrace the beautiful woman.

Oh, God. She really is his girlfriend. Of course she is. Tristan looked perfect with Celia. It was obvious they were a couple. A couple of beautiful, sophisticated people. Like a pair of models from a Burberry ad.

She'd never had a snowball's chance in hell with a guy like him.

Kat slipped away, her pint of Nelson's Revenge in her hands as she left Tristan and headed back to her friends. Mark and Lacy were watching her when she dropped down into her seat and covered her face with her hand.

"Wow, Kat, that was..." Lacy reached out and gave Kat's shoulder a pat.

"Mortifying? Pathetic?" Kat supplied, as she finally dropped her hand from her face and set her glass down next to Mark, nudging it in his direction. Drinking the pint seemed to pale in comparison to the adventure of being kissed by Tristan Kingsley.

"Well, the kiss was kind of hot...until that other girl showed up," Mark observed with a smirk, but he had a point.

She'd been totally on fire and hadn't wanted to stop kissing Tristan. It was as though her life had depended on touching him, on feeling his muscles move beneath her hands, and his mouth exploring hers. There had been nothing else in the world she'd wanted more than him in that moment. She'd *never* felt like that before about anyone or anything.

"I know, right? What kind of guy kisses someone like that when he has a girlfriend?" Lacy said, crossing her arms over her chest.

Mark laughed. "Obviously that guy."

Kat winced. "Do you mind if I just go back to the dorm? I think I've had enough of this place tonight."

"But it's your birthday." Lacy pouted.

Kat shrugged. This was the first time she wasn't celebrating with her father. They'd moved from Chicago to London in August and neither of them had thought about what it would mean when she was two hours away at Cambridge for her birthday. Somehow celebrating without him didn't feel right.

"What about cake?" Mark asked before drinking some of his pint.

"No, thanks." Kat shook her head and brushed some dust off the table, avoiding looking in Tristan's direction.

How was it possible to still feel his lips on hers when he was a dozen feet away?

"Are you sure?" Lacy asked, her brows knit together in concern.

"Yeah, I'm sure. I'd rather just go back to the dorms. I have a lot of studying ahead of me in the next couple of weeks before final exams."

"Well, drat," Lacy said. "All right, you go home, then." She nudged Mark. "Go pay for the drinks. It's on us tonight, Kat."

"Thanks, guys." Kat stood and tucked her chair under the wooden table. "See you both tomorrow?"

"Bright and early," Lacy laughed. "Did I ever say how much I hate 8:30 a.m. classes?"

Mark leaned over and kissed Lacy's cheek. "That's why I'm the smart one. My first class is never before 11 a.m."

"That's right, rub it in," Lacy grumbled, but she was smiling at him.

"Bye, guys." Kat was still laughing as she exited the pub. She didn't want to think about the mysterious Tristan Kingsley or how he kissed. Better to just forget it and move on. It had been a fun adventure, even if a short one.

The snow blew in thick currents around her, and the dim streetlights looked like glowing golden orbs in the darkness. It was a bewitching sight.

Most of the small shops around the pub were closed, but one was still open. Its merry lights called to her as she approached. A bakery. Cakes, breads, and other sweets filled the windows. Behind the glass counter, a plump woman was checking a tray of cookies, the front of her blue apron dusted with small white splotches of flour.

"Maybe just one," Kat murmured, entranced by the sight of the small chocolate cupcakes with elaborate swirls of icing. It was her birthday, after all. Kat entered the shop and the brass bell above her head tinkled.

"Hello, dearie," the woman said and wiped flour-covered hands on her apron. "Come to get a late-night snack? You're just in time, I was ready to close up early due to the weather."

Kat peered through the glass cases, trying to decide which one of the little cakes would taste as good as the man she'd kissed only minutes ago. She doubted anything could come close.

Tristan. Tristan who had a girlfriend. Kat mentally kicked herself. She'd pretty much thrown herself at him and begged to be kissed. Maybe he didn't normally go around slipping his tongue between a girl's lips and setting her on fire inside. Then again...if he'd been a good guy, he wouldn't have done more than a chaste peck on the cheek.

Focus on chocolate, not hot Brit you'll never see again. She went back to studying the contents of the case. When the entry bell clinked again, she didn't turn around.

"Have a need for something sweet?" A rich, decadent voice, smooth as chocolate, filled her ears.

She spun to find Tristan standing there, snow dancing about him as he let the door close behind him. He walked toward her with lithe, graceful steps. Her body trembled with a little wave of excitement at the mere sight of him. *I shouldn't be happy to see him, he has a girlfriend...*But that didn't change the rapid beat of her heart.

"Evening," the baker said merrily.

"What are you doing here?" Kat sputtered. The

moment the words were out, she slapped a hand over her mouth.

His chuckle made a warm flush creep down her cheeks. "I saw you left the pub and..." He paused, his brows drawing together. "Well, I didn't want you to go off on your own. I saw that your friends remained behind." It was a lame excuse, and they both knew it. For some reason that made her want to smile.

"So you're protecting me from snowflakes?" She couldn't help the partly amused and partly sarcastic tone of her voice.

Tristan shrugged and joined her at the counter, peering at the desserts. "Snowflakes can be treacherous buggers."

This time she couldn't stop her laugh. "I'll bet. Death by ice fractals sounds horrifying."

He quirked a brow. "Ice fractals?"

God, I'm an idiot. Sure, Kat, show him what a nerd you are. "They're the mathematical phenomena of a repeating pattern that displays on every scale. Snowflakes are one of nature's fractals." She wasn't a science wiz, but learning was something she enjoyed, no matter what subject. Ben had always teased her about it. Not that she'd minded being called a nerd. There were worse things than being addicted to learning.

Tristan glanced over his shoulder at the dancing snow, then turned back to her. "I'm surprised you know what fractals are. Most people don't." He leaned forward then and caught a lock of her hair, playing with the strands. Kat held her breath as every nerve in her tingled to life. He was touching her again, and she could feel every cell of her body humming with excitement.

Please kiss me again.

When he didn't, her mind attempted to return to reality, and she remembered Celia.

"What about your girlfriend?" she blurted out.

"Girlfriend?" He let her hair drop from his fingers and met her gaze.

"That woman in the pub..." *The one he looked so perfect standing next to.*

"Celia?" The responding smile that lit his face filled her with envy. Would a man ever smile like that when he thought about her? Something about Tristan and the way he smiled, she couldn't help but wish one smile was for her.

"Right, Celia," she echoed. Her heart twinged a little at the mention of the other woman.

"She's my cousin, not my girlfriend."

Kat stared. This total stranger had abandoned his cousin to chase after her? Tiny flutters of excitement stirred in her stomach.

"You seem surprised." His sensual lips—lips she couldn't get out of her mind—twitched, as though he was fighting off a smile.

"Why ditch your cousin when you don't even know me?" This entire evening was surreal. God-like men coming in from snowstorms to kiss her sense-less...What next? Winning the lottery and moving to the Bahamas?

Tristan's gaze dropped to her mouth.

"When a lovely woman kisses me and runs off into the snowy night...well, the temptation to go after her is irresistible. I don't let lovely women es-cape, not until I've tasted them properly." He licked his lips and everything south of her waist throbbed to life.

What? Was he kidding?

"So here I am, in a bakery with you. Is there a reason we're staring at cakes?" He moved a step closer, even though he was facing the desserts again.

His arm brushed her right shoulder. The man was tall, but not too tall. Just enough to make a girl feel small, in a good way, like he could protect her if she needed it. A masculine scent, warm and clean, filled her nose. *His* scent. It was an enticing one she could've inhaled forever.

Focus, Kat. Try to be normal and have a normal conversation. Do not keep starting at Mr. Sexy.

"It's my birthday today. I'm nineteen."

At her reply, he looked at her again.

"Well, we must get you a cake. Chocolate, I presume?" He leaned one elbow on the glass counter as he waited for her to answer.

She nodded mutely.

Tristan turned back to the woman behind the counter. "What's the best chocolate cake you have? The richest, most decadent one." His words were as decadent as his statement. She could practically feel the chocolate melting on her tongue.

"The Devil's Triple Layer Cake." The woman pulled out a small cake for two people. Raspberry sauce was drizzled over the top of the simple yet elegant icing design.

Tristan took out his wallet and slid a black credit card across the counter.

"We'll take it. And a small candle, if you have one."

"But—" Kat's protest died when the woman took the Devil's cake from the counter and started to box it up. She didn't like feeling indebted to him, and he'd already made her feel off balance with his kisses.

"Consider it a thank-you." He laughed.

"For what?" Her tone was a breathless as she watched his dark hair fall into his eyes. Her hands twitched to brush it back from his face, to touch him back the way he'd so boldly touched her earlier. Everything about this man drew her in—his face, his eyes, his rich voice speaking of kisses and passion.

"You surprised me tonight. It's been a long time since anyone has done that." He scrubbed a hand over his jaw, and she saw the hint of stubble there and remembered the way it had tickled her when she'd kissed him.

I surprised myself, kissing him like that.

"Allow me to escort you home. Is it a long walk?" Tristan asked Kat, when the woman had returned with the boxed cake.

"Only a block. I'm staying in a dorm at Magdalene College." She shouldn't be telling him something like that. What if he got the wrong idea?

"A student at university? Excellent. So am I." He

smiled. "I'm not an undergraduate, though. I'm earning a Master's degree in business." He thanked the baker and collected the box with the cake. "I'll walk you home." It was a statement this time, not a question, and she didn't want to argue with him, not when it meant spending more time in his presence. She'd just have to be sure he didn't think she'd...well, she'd worry about that when they got to her dorm.

"You're a student? How old are you?" Kat could've smacked herself for being so rude. "I'm sorry, I shouldn't have asked."

"I'm twenty-five." He held the door open with one hand, and she had to slide past him to exit the bakery. A gust carrying fresh snow hit her face, and she braced against the frigid air. Her first instinct was to turn around and bury herself against Tristan. He was so warm, she remembered from kissing him at the bar. The way his body had enveloped hers with heat, and the way his hands had gripped her hips.

"So what brings an American to Cambridge? Is this a semester of study abroad?" He walked alongside her as they went down the street, snow crunching beneath their feet. Kat stayed closer to Tristan than she would have normally, telling herself it was because she was afraid she'd slip on the ice. But the truth was that she wanted to be close to him, feel his warmth, smell that piney scent of his that made her senses come alive. She struggled to focus on their conversation, given how her thoughts kept drifting into dangerous territory.

"I'm a full-time student. My father travels for work, and he's living in London for the next couple of years."

Tristan made a little hum of interest. "And what does your father do?"

"He's an investment banker at Barclays. He's at their London office, and I wanted to be close to him." It was so easy to talk to Tristan. Maybe it was because

sity only seemed to deepen as the snowfall muffled the world around them. Like they were cocooned in the shelter of a snow globe holding only them and the falling white flakes.

She licked her lips. "Yes. For a long time now."

Tristan nodded. "My parents are divorced, as well. My father is an overbearing, pompous arse." He chuckled, but there was a bite to the sound that caught her attention.

"You don't like your father?" she asked.

The flash of cold in his eyes made her shiver more than the snow falling around them. He continued to stroke her cheek with one of his hands, which softened the hard look in his eyes.

"I don't like to talk about him." It was clear from the steel in his voice that she wouldn't get anything else from him about his father. But she wanted to know more about this mysterious, seductive stranger whose kisses burned straight through her. There were hidden depths to him, dark, deep, flowing underground rivers and she wanted to dive in and discover who he really was.

"What about your mother?"

The defensiveness evaporated as he grinned. "One of the best, as far as mothers go."

"That must be nice, to have a mother around, I mean." A part of her still felt like maybe *she* had been the cause of her parents' breakup. Maybe she'd been too much for her mother to handle.

"It's not your fault, you know. Sometimes it feels like it is, but it isn't." His hand on her cheek moved to her hair, threading through the wild strands that were slightly damp with melted snow. The heat in his eyes burned slowly, like a fire in a hearth.

Kat's body responded, her thighs clenching together and her nipples hardening. From a single hot, tender look, she was melting for this intense, handsome stranger. A shiver racked her, and he chuckled.

Did he know how much he was affecting her? He had to, with that pleased look gleaming in his eyes, and his lips twitching in bemusement.

"Let's get you inside so you can warm up and eat your birthday cake."

She came back to herself and realized they'd been standing inside the courtyard, unmoving, just standing so close, breaths mingled and almost whispering as they opened up about their lives.

They walked up to the front of the red brick dormitory, and he followed her up the small set of steps to her door on the first floor. She turned, ready to thank him for walking her home, but he caught the door, preventing it from shutting.

"May I come inside?" He tilted his head toward the door, and she saw he was still carrying the cake.

"I..." she swallowed down the nervous lump in her throat. She wasn't ready to say good night, or good-bye. But she didn't want him thinking she was the sort of girl who slept with someone she just met. He seemed to sense her indecision.

"Just for cake," he said. "You have my gentleman's promise." He used his index finger to draw a cross over his heart.

A gentleman's promise? She remembered the things those girls had said back in the pub. Was he the sort of man to break a promise? Or just a girl's heart?

Take a chance, a little voice whispered inside her head. *He's a risk worth taking, at least tonight.* If she did let him inside, she'd get to spend more time with him. She didn't want to let him out of her sight, not until she'd figured him out. She'd always loved puzzles, and this strange, sexy man was more of a puzzle than anything she'd ever seen.

"Okay. But just for a few minutes." She let him follow her inside. It was large for a dormitory room, with a tiny kitchen counter against one wall and a small bathroom. Flicking on the one overhead light, she took the bakery box from Tristan and set it on her desk before turning around to face him. She couldn't help but wonder what he'd think of the world she'd built in the few short months she'd lived here.

The walls were a pale, eggshell white, and she'd covered most of them with posters of famous British people. Tristan eyed one above her bed.

"Lord Nelson? Good God, that sure explains your drink tonight at the Pickerel." He burst out laughing. "What is it like to wake up to that each morning?" The rich sound of his amusement warmed her insides all over again, and she started laughing, too.

"My father got it for me as a joke, and I loved it. I thought he deserved a place of honor."

The throaty laugh that escaped his lips was husky this time. "Above a woman's bed is certainly a place of honor." His gaze roved over her full-sized bed, with its dark royal blue and white fleur-de-lis pattern.

Simple and elegant. *Just like him. He'd look so good on my bed.* The thought made her blush.

It was the first time she'd really let herself go there. When she'd dated in high school, she'd never let herself think about sex. It was pointless to build that connection with someone when her father might be transferred to a new location at any time, and they'd have to pack up their lives again. But she wasn't going to be moving for the next three years. Maybe now was the time to give it a chance.

Tristan stripped off his coat and laid it over the back of her desk chair. She had a brief moment to admire his body from behind, the lean lines of his legs, the broad, muscular shoulders outlined by his sweater, before he would notice her staring. The man was gorgeous. Too gorgeous. It was intimidating, yet she didn't want to look away.

She was still staring when he straightened and

faced her. Oh, what he could do to her with that body...Tristan was making her feel a little crazy. Okay, really crazy. She wanted to touch him, to put her hands on his chest, feel that heat she remembered from the pub, and kiss him again. God, she wanted to kiss him, and it almost made her hurt with hunger.

"How about we taste that cake?" He grinned almost lazily, as if he'd known she'd been thinking sinful thoughts.

"Uh...right." She dug through her cabinet and found a pair of blue plates, a knife, and two forks. She cut two slices and held one out to him.

He didn't take his plate right away, instead reaching into the bag from the bakery and retrieving the little packet of candles. He nestled one on the top of her slice.

"You don't need to—"

"Of course I do." He produced a small lighter with a silver crest embossed on it and flicked it on, the flame sparking as he put it to the wick of the candle. The crest matched the one engraved on the gold signet ring on his left hand.

Another part of the mystery. What sort of man wore a signet ring? Given what she knew about history, especially English history, she had to wonder if he might be...No that was silly. He couldn't be royalty. She knew enough about the current monarchy to know he wasn't related to Prince William or Prince Harry. Was he titled? A lord? If so, what was he doing studying at Cambridge? It wasn't unusual for nobles to send their children to study at Oxford or Cambridge, but after they'd gotten their undergraduate degree they didn't normally pursue graduate studies. Of course, the simpler explanation was that he was simply wearing the ring as a fashion statement. A lot of British movie stars wore signet rings to give themselves an aura of mystery.

"What's the symbol on your ring?" she asked, nodding at his hand.

A shadow flickered across his eyes, and he glanced away before he replied. "A family heirloom."

That only created a hundred other questions, but she was prevented from asking anything else because he'd successfully lit the candle.

Once the wick caught fire and burned steadily, he pocketed the lighter and took the plate from her hands.

"Now make a wish and blow it out." Tristan's eyes locked with hers, and that enchanting blue-green was now bright with fire. They were so close, only the plate separating them, as he watched her, waiting.

She leaned down, closed her eyes.

I wish... What did she wish for? A funny thought popped into her head, and she felt strange enough to go with it.

I wish to have an adventure. She was tired of reading about them between the pages of old books, she wanted to live one. Standing here with Tristan and kissing him tonight was the start, and she wanted more, so much more. With a puff, she blew out the candle, and smoke curled up from the blackened tip of the wick.

"Happy birthday, Kat," Tristan whispered.

"Thank you." Kat meant for more than just his sweet words. She meant for the cake, for the kiss in the pub, for setting her down a path of living. She flicked her gaze up to his again as she removed the candle from the slice of cake and set it aside on the counter.

A slow smile curved his lips as he handed back her plate and collected his own. Then he walked over to her bed and sat down.

Tristan tasted his cake, and she wished he were tasting her. She wanted to be back in his arms, kissing him. And part of her was curious to know what made him so notorious that women were whispering about him in pubs.

I have to be smart about this. There was no way she could ask him to kiss her again and open that door to more intimacy. Not after he'd made a promise to behave like a gentleman and just eat his cake. But she was torn. Wanting him to stay, wanting more, and being afraid of that desire and where it could lead. After just a short while of being around him, she could see that heartbreaker side to him, the one that would hurt her if she fell for him. He was full of charm, sex appeal, and mystery. There wasn't a woman in the world who wasn't intrigued by that, or seduced by that...

"Mmm...The baker wasn't lying. This cake is sinful." He patted the bedside next to him. "Come sit."

Kat tried to ignore her confusion about Tristan and the way he made her feel. Hesitant, excited, off balance, fascinated. He was too handsome to be in her room and on her bed. And his simple presence on her bed made her mind go to wonderful places. The images he put in her head with just a thought should have scared her. She wanted to do things with him that she'd never thought about before. Like having him push her flat onto her back and pin her wrists on either side of her head while he kissed her, ruthless, seductive, hard, as she wriggled beneath him, desperate for more. His eyes promised that and so much more as he licked his lips and watched her.

She was finally nineteen, but he made her want to be twenty-five, worldly and experienced. Being around Tristan, she wanted to be someone interesting. Which brought her back to a question that plagued her: Was he pretending to be interested, wanting another notch on his bedpost and thinking she'd be an easy target?

Or does he really like me? A nervous flutter stirred in her stomach again.

"Why did you really follow me to the bakery?" she asked.

For a man like him to come after her when the pub had been filled with plenty of pretty college girls, there had to be a reason. She wasn't exactly the type of girl guys flocked after. She was a size twelve, definitely curvy, with brown hair and gray eyes. Not a stunning model or even like the prettier girls she'd seen on campus, those tall leggy British beauties who were similar to his cousin Celia.

Tristan bit into a forkful of cake, sucking chocolate off the prongs.

Kat stared at his mouth, remembering all too well how his lips had felt on hers.

"You've caught my attention, Kat." He set his plate on the table by the bed and folded his arms over his chest.

"Your attention?" She avoided the bed and sat at her desk, where she nibbled on the cake. The flavors were decadent. The zing of the raspberry, the dark, almost erotic taste of the semi-sweet chocolate. *Sinful*.

"Yes." He reached up to stroke his jaw. "Very few things attract my attention. But *you* did." His brows drew together.

What did that mean? Kat had trouble swallowing. Maybe if she drank something...Kneeling by her fridge, she retrieved a small carton of milk.

"Want something to drink?" she offered.

"Yes. Thank you." He rose from the bed and came up behind her. The warmth of his body seared hers as he reached around her to grab one of her mugs and fill it himself.

A shiver rippled down her spine, and she closed her eyes a brief moment, until he stepped back again. Then she raised her glass to her lips and hastily drank, trying to quench the thirst chocolate always created, and this newer thirst for the man not two feet from her. He was like a drug—one hit and she needed more. To feel that giddy rush when he pinned her against a wall, his hands exploring her curves, his mouth possessing hers...She was supposed to be playing it cool, and not letting him think he could get her into bed, at least not tonight. The fact that this was exactly what she wanted was very...very bad.

OTHER TITLES BY LAUREN
SMITH

Historical
The League of Rogues Series
Wicked Designs
His Wicked Seduction
Her Wicked Proposal
Wicked Rivals
Her Wicked Longing
His Wicked Embrace
The Earl of Pembroke
His Wicked Secret
The Last Wicked Rogue
Never Kiss a Scot (Coming Spring 2019)
The Earl of Kent (Coming Fall 2019)
The Seduction Series
The Duelist's Seduction
The Rakehell's Seduction
The Rogue's Seduction
The Gentleman's Seduction
Standalone Stories
Tempted by A Rogue
Sins and Scandals
An Earl By Any Other Name
A Gentleman Never Surrenders
A Scottish Lord for Christmas

Contemporary
The Surrender Series
The Gilded Cuff
The Gilded Cage
The Gilded Chain
The Darkest Hour
Love In London
Forbidden
Seduction
Climax
Forever Be Mine

Paranormal
Dark Seductions Series
The Shadows of Stormclyffe Hall
The Love Bites Series
The Bite of Winter
Brothers of Ash and Fire
Grigori
Mikhail
Rurik
The Lost Barinov Dragon (Coming Soon)

Sci-Fi Romance
Cyborg Genesis Series
Across the Stars
The Krinar World of Anna Zaires
The Krinar Eclipse (Coming Soon!)

USA TODAY Bestselling Author Lauren Smith is an Oklahoma attorney by day, who pens adventurous and edgy romance stories by the light of her smart phone flashlight app. She knew she was destined to be a romance writer when she attempted to re-write the entire *Titanic* movie just to save Jack from drowning. Connecting with readers by writing emotionally moving, realistic and sexy romances no matter what time period is her passion. She's won multiple awards in several romance sub-genres including: New England Reader's Choice Awards, Greater Detroit BookSeller's Best Awards, and a Semi-Finalist award for the Mary Wollstonecraft Shelley Award.

To connect with Lauren, visit her at:
www.laurensmithbooks.com
lauren@Laurensmithbooks.com

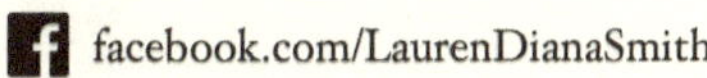 facebook.com/LaurenDianaSmith

twitter.com/LSmithAuthor

instagram.com/LaurenSmithbooks

 bookbub.com/authors/lauren-smith